The Hand of Doume

Elizabeth Pewsey was born in Chile to a South American mother and an English father – her Argentinian grandmother was a poet and, she says, 'as nutty as a fruitcake'! Both parents were writers and great travellers, and she lived in India as a child before the family settled in Britain, where she finished her schooling and went to Oxford University. She now lives in Dorset with her husband and two children. Elizabeth Pewsey is the author of *The Talking Head* trilogy.

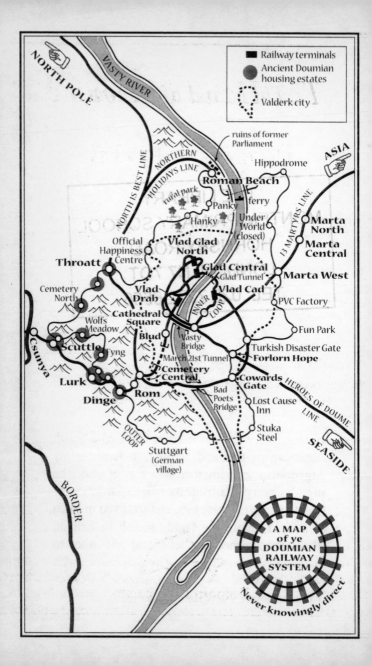

The Hand of Doume

Elizabeth Pewsey

Dolphin Paperbacks

Other books by Elizabeth Pewsey
The Talking Head
The Dewstone Quest
The Walled City

First published in Great Britain in 1999
as a Dolphin paperback
by Orion Children's Books
a division of the Orion Publishing Group Ltd
Orion House
5 Upper St Martin's Lane
London WC2H 9EA

A catalogue record for this book
is available from the British Library.

Typeset at The Spartan Press Ltd,
Lymington, Hants
Printed in Great Britain by
Clays Ltd, St Ives plc.

ISBN 1 85881 545 2

For Paddy Robinson, comrade in anarchy

Hand stolen

KNIGHT OF DOUME
LOSES LIMB

A hand has been severed at the wrist and removed from the body of a knight of Doume.

These famously preserved bodies lie in the gloom of the Cathedral of St Vlad the Good in Valderk, capital city of the Kingdom of Doume.

The police are treating the crime as a major one, and because it is a matter of State Security, the Chief of Secret Police is on the case. Chief Stuka declined to be questioned last night, but claimed to be on the track of the criminals already.

The knight who lost his hand was Baldwin the Odd, one of the original knights who came to Doume when he got lost on the way to the Crusades.

Our medic writes:

These bodies have been perfectly preserved for hundreds of years in the special air of the cathedral. It is a mystery to science why this happens, although some experts think is has to do with the quantity of herb-laced liquors consumed by the knights while they were alive.

One

I'T'S DIFFERENT IN THE KINGDOM OF DOUME.
You've probably never heard of the Kingdom of
Doume. I hadn't, either, until I came home from school
and Mum broke the news that we were going there. And
not for a holiday, either; as it turned out, nobody would
go to Doume for a holiday. On account of it being so
different – it takes a lot longer than two weeks in a coach
to get used to Doume and the Doumians.

Up till a quarter past four, it had been a perfectly
ordinary day. School, boring, boring, as always on a
Thursday, on account of double maths, double geography followed by religious studies; well, you get the
picture.

So I wasn't entirely in a joyous mood when I got
home. It was raining hard, great sheets of water
pelting down out of a muddy grey sky. Quite a lot of
the water seemed to be trickling down my nose and
down the back of my neck; that didn't help my mood.
I checked in the hall mirror, yes, just as I guessed. I
looked like a drowned beast. I slung my bag along the
floor and it landed up against the radiator, like it
always does.

Mum said, 'Don't do that,' like she always does, and
Wilf said, 'Hey, guess what, we're going to live in the
Kingdom of Doume.'

Wilf is my brother. He's younger than I am; not

much, but enough for me to pull rank. 'What are you talking about?' I said.

Mum wasn't pleased. 'Wilf, I told you that I'd tell Beanbag myself.'

Beanbag is me. No, it's not the name on my birth certificate. My real name is Beatrice, after my auntie Bea, who's completely nuts. Nobody really liked the name Beatrice, and my dad, so they tell me, used to carry me around slumped on his shoulder like a beanbag, and the name stuck. I like it. It's individual and personal.

'You'd hum and ha and beat around the bush, and she wouldn't have a clue what you were on about,' Wilf told Mum.

Wilf is very astute for one of his tender years.

'Much better to break the awful news straight off.'

'Kingdom of Doume?' I said. 'You aren't serious. There's no such place.'

'There is,' said Wilf. 'And we're going to live there.'

'Not me,' I said at once. If there's one thing I hate, it's being pushed around. Parents picking you up and dumping you in terra incognita, such as this Kingdom of Doume place, counted as being pushed around.

'Actually,' said Wilf, 'I'm not going either.' He was munching on some chocolate spread accompanied by a little toast, and wasn't speaking very clearly. Still, I got the gist. 'I'm going to be in the chess team next term,' he went on indistinctly.

Wilf is an intellectual.

'Listen,' said Mum, in that teeth-clenched way adults have when they think they're being reasonable. 'Listen. Your father has to go to Doume. For his work. He is going for some time. I am going with him. So are you.'

'People whose parents go abroad to strange places leave their kids in boarding schools.' I'd always rather liked the idea of boarding school, feasts in the dorm, persecuting the French mistress. You know the scenario.

Mum went pale. 'No way am I leaving you in a boarding school. I know what goes on there. Besides, we'd miss you.'

'No, you wouldn't,' said Wilf, licking the corners of his mouth to get the last atoms of chocolate on to his tongue. 'Think how peaceful it would be without us.'

'There is that,' said Mum.

What a nerve! 'If you don't want us there, then of course we'll come,' I said. 'Where is this place, anyhow? It isn't a desert island by any chance, is it?'

Wilf sighed. 'What work would Dad do on a desert island?'

Good point, but one can always hope. 'Okay, know-all, tell us about Doume.'

'It's in Europe,' said Wilf, sliding across the floor to the shelf where the big books live. 'Sort of in the middle.'

He riffled through the pages and then laid the atlas down flat on the table. 'There,' he said.

'Oh, there,' I said, as though I was well acquainted with that part of the world, which I certainly am not.

'It was founded by some English knights in the twelfth century,' Wilf went on. 'They were a cowardly lot, who thought the Crusades were a bit strenuous, all that fighting and besieging and so on. So they peeled off and wandered about until they came to Doume. They thought it looked a good sort of place, where nobody would find them, so they stayed.'

I didn't believe a word of it. 'A likely story. What about the people who were already there? Bet they wouldn't have put up with a lot of knights taking up residence.'

'They didn't mind the knights. They thought the knights would protect them.'

'It sounds very fanciful to me,' I said. 'How do you know all this?'

'A girl in my class did a project on Doume. Mind you, the teacher thought she'd made it all up.'

'Only she hadn't.'

'No, as we now know.' Wilf closed the atlas and slid back to the shelf with it. Wilf is like that, very tidy about books and things.

I hate abroad. 'It'll be full of foreigners,' I said. 'All speaking a language we don't understand.'

Mum had retreated to the kitchen, but she heard that. 'The language will be all right. They mostly speak English. On account of the knights, I expect. So school won't be a problem.'

School! In another country. I felt really depressed.

Mum came out of the kitchen with chunks of ginger cake to cheer us up. 'Those knights are supposed to ride through the central square of the capital city once a year,' she said brightly.

Wilf and I looked at each other. 'They're dead, Mum,' he said in a kindly voice. 'The knights were there a long time ago, like eight centuries or so.'

'Their ghosts are supposed to ride, I should have said.'

Wilf tapped his forehead, and I clicked my tongue sympathetically. 'It's the shock,' I said.

Mum was back in the kitchen. 'It's in the guidebook I bought.'

Eek.

That was when I knew this was for real. This Doume trip was going to happen. Why? Because Mum never bought guidebooks. We hardly ever went on holiday, because Dad works for himself, he's what's called a freelance operator. If he takes a holiday, he doesn't get paid. When we did go away, Mum borrowed a guide-book from the library.

Buying meant serious.

THE DARKSIDE GUIDE TO
THE KINGDOM OF DOUME

Notable Doumians

KING VLAD XXIII

Inherited the throne as a child from his father, Vlad XXII, Vlad the Flab. Unlike his late father, the current King is lean and fit. He lost the crown when the communists came to power, converted to their cause, and until regaining the crown seven years ago, worked in the bell-testing depart-ment in The People's Bicycle Factory (formerly Vurke's Volcanic Velocipedes or VVV).

It is from this that he acquired the title 'Comrade Vlad.'

He retains his affection for bicycles by using a royal bicycle as his main official transport – not a popular choice as far as his officials are concerned, since they are also expected to use government-issue black 'Magpie' bikes whenever possible. Comrade Vlad married Venetia Vurke, daughter of the founder of the bicycle factory, whom he met while he was on secondment to the brake section where she was sent after the factory was confiscated and the family denounced. They have three children and currently reside in Castle Bane.

Two

'WHAT WE CAN'T TAKE, CAN'T LEAVE AND DON'T want to store, is off to the dump.'

Dad was being efficient.

'Poor Humphrey,' said Wilf.

'Don't be silly,' said Mum, dropping all the cushions she'd just picked up, and saying something very rude under her breath. 'Of course I don't mean Humphrey.'

Humphrey was the cat. He was going to lodge with some cousins, and although Wilf knew that Humphrey would be one happy cat on a Welsh farm, he was going to miss him.

'I expect they eat cats in Doume,' I said. 'When I said I was moving to Doume, a girl in my class told me her uncle went there on a trip. It sent him round the bend, and after he came back he had to spend three months in a clinic.'

It was only about a fortnight after Mum had dropped her bombshell, and here we were, packing. 'We're renting a furnished place there,' Dad said. 'You'll have to pack your own things. Don't leave it all to Mum.'

Wilf had no problems. He put his violin in a pile together with his music case, a music stand, his favourite books, the shabby seal which accompanied him everywhere, and a box of pencils.

Dad looked at Wilf's pile. 'Clothes might be a good

idea,' he said. 'And you'll want some books. I'm not sure Doumian television is up to much.'

'Hope they show *Star Trek*,' said Wilf, seriously worried.

'They show *Star Trek* everywhere,' I told him. 'When we get to Mars, the Martians will all be sitting round watching Captain Kirk and wittering on about space warps.'

Dad had got hold of an official leaflet about Doume, published by the government to brief visiting officials and businessmen. 'This is the real lowdown,' said Dad. 'None of your touristy bumpf here. Just hard facts.'

You could tell it wasn't for tourists, nobody would produce anything as dull-looking as that if they actually wanted to encourage you to go somewhere. I pointed this out to Dad, and he said they were all like that, even the ones to places like Spain and Italy. 'Hard facts for serious travellers,' he said approvingly. Dad isn't taken in by appearances, as you can see.

Wilf and I took it off to our hut in the garden.

I have to tell you, this serious travellers' guide was a real eye-opener. I mean, you do geography and all that at school, but it's just drains and social this-and-that in some distant country. It might as well be ancient Rome; it doesn't affect you, you aren't ever going to go there.

But we were.

'Currency,' read out Wilf. 'The perk, which is divided into one hundred erks.'

'At least it's decimals.' Some countries don't have decimal currencies, did you know that? Imagine the sums at school.

'The old currency, the vlad, exists side-by-side with the perk. The vlad is worth approximately three and a half perks. Twenty fangs make one vlad, and fangs are further divided into twelve phillings.'

'I don't like the sound of that at all,' I said, thinking of those sums.

'Climate,' announced Wilf. 'Central European. Cold and often snowy in winter. Mild, short springs, and hot summers, often with very little rain, especially in the plains. The weather near the mountains, around Lake Snood and in the Forest of Doume is variable.'

'Oh, very helpful.'

Wilf had switched to his radio announcer's drone. 'Cities. The capital city is Valderk. This is the political, administrative and cultural centre of Doume.'

'That's where we're going to live.'

'Warning to travellers: Valderk is not a safe city after dark.'

'What?' That sounded alarming. Not safe? Muggers? Wild drivers? Mad rapists?

'Why?'

'It doesn't say.'

'Let me see.' I took charge of the guide. I had this feeling that Wilf was making it all up.

He wasn't, and I didn't like what I was reading; I didn't like it at all. 'Listen. Travellers are advised to pack toilet paper, matches and candles and soap. It is also advisable to bring bath plugs.'

'Did you say bath plugs?'

'Yes.'

Wilf thought about that. 'Perhaps they only take showers.'

'Perhaps they haven't had the lectures on personal hygiene.'

'Perhaps we'd better stay put.'

Three

N O CHANCE.

Three days later, we were sitting on a plane which was cruising at 30,000 feet towards Doume.

I haven't travelled a lot by plane, but you didn't need to be a frequent flyer to know that this plane was a dodgy specimen. And no safety notices in the seat pockets, as Wilf pointed out. No seat pockets in which to put safety notices, in fact. And the stewardess spent the whole flight crouched in her seat as though we were about to plunge into the sea.

'We should have flown British Airways,' said Mum.

'They don't fly to Doume. That's why we're on Royal Doumian.' Dad was getting snappy, which is unusual for him. A calm man, my father.

'We shall be landing shortly at Vlad the Cad airport,' announced a crackly voice. 'Please extinguish your cigarettes and fasten your seat belts.'

'Very shortly,' said Dad breathlessly, as the plane bounced down on to the ground. It had a serious tilt, and the overhead lockers flew open and bags hurtled about the plane as it roared down the runway and juddered to a violent halt.

The tall man in the seat across the aisle rubbed his head and picked up some of the things from the lockers. 'They're in a hurry because of the bats,' he said.

★

Bats, indeed. What bats?

We were standing on a chilly, windswept tarmac, waiting for the bus to take us to the terminal. At least, not exactly waiting for the bus, because the bus was there, only with all its doors closed. The driver, a stout individual with a big droopy black moustache, was in his seat, but he appeared to be fast asleep.

I looked across to the distant outline of some hills. Were those bats? Those black creatures flitting to and fro in the fading light of dusk? 'They're quite big bats,' I said, trying to sound nonchalant.

'Enormous,' said the man. 'Give you a nasty nip, I can tell you. The planes can't take off once they start circling the airport.'

I didn't feel too happy about those bats. 'Is Valderk near here?' I asked him.

'Valderk's in that direction. Miles away. I can never work out why they built this airport out here, right by a swamp.'

'Swamp?'

'Marshy land, anyhow,' said the man. 'Can't you hear the frogs?'

I could, now he mentioned it.

'What with them and the bats squeaking and things howling . . .'

'Things?'

'You know.'

I didn't, but thought it best not to ask.

'Valderk is hilly on one side of the river and completely flat on the other. Which side are you staying on?'

Dad didn't know. 'Dread Street,' he said doubtfully.

'Oh, that's a classy district. It's on the hilly side.'

The driver had by now woken up, and he slouched over to open the door of the bus.

'Are we the only passengers who've got off the plane?'

Dad asked the tall man, looking around the empty seats in surprise.

'Yes. They'll pick up those lucky folk who are leaving Doume, and then the plane goes on to Budapest. Lucky them; I wish I were going on to Budapest.'

The bus rumbled, backfired several times, and jolted into movement.

'Do you live here?' Mum asked politely.

'For the moment, yes,' said the man regretfully.

Being nosy, I asked what he was doing in Doume, since he didn't seem too keen on the place.

'I'm a trade adviser,' he said, not sounding very enthusiastic about his work. 'Soft drinks and confectionery. My grandmother came from Doume, so the firm thought I was the right person for the job.'

'Don't you like it here?' asked Wilf.

The man turned his eyes up in a dramatic way. Effective, I'd like to be able to do that. 'It kind of takes some getting used to, Doume.'

'It's very hot and sticky,' said Wilf.

'The guidebook said it would be,' said Mum, dripping.

I lugged my bag up the steps into the terminal; Doume didn't seem to have heard of trolleys or escalators. The arrivals hall didn't improve one's morale, either, being a dingy hangar-type place, no posters, no shops, just twenty-watt light bulbs hanging from wires.

A grim person with dark stubble and a khaki uniform demanded our passports and then disappeared with them.

'Look,' said Wilf, standing on the luggage carousel so that he could look out of the clear part of the windows. 'They're piling new passengers into the plane like anything. Wow, they've already shut the doors.'

'There aren't many flights,' said Dad, looking at the board as the roar of the plane readying itself for take-off rang round the gloomy hall.

I peered at the Arrivals and Departures board. 'That isn't the plane we were on. It says the one leaving now is going to Paris.'

'No flights to or from Paris any more,' said our fellow passenger. He took out a large spotted handkerchief and mopped his brow. 'They stopped over a year ago. Those flight details have been up there for as long as I can remember.'

'I see,' said Dad.

'Are you on holiday?' asked the man.

'Wish we were,' I said. 'Looks to me like a fortnight here would be fourteen days too long.'

'I'll see you around then, I expect,' said the man. 'My name's Johnson. Good luck. And don't worry. You'll get used to it. In time.'

'Used to what?' asked Wilf, with foreboding.

The Shout of Doume

Artworks stolen by aliens claims clairvoyant

Mystic Miklos says he has seen in his crystal ball tall, purple beings with insect-like heads bearing the treasures of Doume to a waiting spacecraft. He claims that several monks were being dragged along as well.

What are the police doing about this? Have they been out to the spot where four great pits in the ground show the spot where the spacecraft landed?

They have not.

Have the families of the monks have been informed of the brother's fate? The answer is no.

Why not? Are they scared of us knowing the truth?

While these alien landings are concealed, no citizen can be safe. We need to have the facts. NO MORE COVER-UPS demands *The Shout*.

Granny eaten by giant cabbage see page 4.

Four

WHEN DAD TOLD US WE WERE TAKING A FURN-
ished flat in Doume, it didn't bother me. I know
all about rented flats. Dad is a security consultant. It
sounds grand, but it isn't. We tease him and call him ex-
cop, because he used to be a policeman, specializing in
protecting galleries and museums and things. Then he
left the force, quite amicably, and set up on his own. So
he goes wherever the work is, and that means we've
moved around quite a lot and have often stayed in
rented places.

Rented flats are all much the same. If you'd asked me
what I'd expected to find in Doume, I'd have said the
sitting room would have a sofa, a couple of fat chairs, a
few boring pictures on the wall. There'd be a TV in the
corner, a table and chairs in the dining room or the
kitchen, pine beds and tacky cupboards in the bed-
room . . .

I couldn't have been more wrong. This place just hit
you between the eyes. 'Wow,' I said.

'Different,' said Wilf, trying to keep his cool.

'Um,' said Dad.

'Henry,' said Mum. 'Is this a joke?'

I prowled past the gothic sofa piled with sinister
cushions embroidered in dark red and purple. The other
chairs in the room were imposing and solid, made of
some black wood and carved with all kinds of patterns

and twiddly bits. The pictures on the walls had castles rising out of gloomy mists and great flights of stone stairs lit by guttering torches. There was an immense fireplace; you could move in and have your friends round to visit in that. It was carved all over with grinning faces and set into it was a very large stove.

'Tiled all over,' said Wilf with awe. 'Look at these weird birds and animals.'

'Very weird,' said Mum with a shudder.

'Sally, come and look at the kitchen,' said Dad in a hopeful voice.

Wilf and I looked at each other as Mum went out of the double doors – another triumph of the woodcarver's art.

A shrill scream rent the air.

'She's going to have hysterics,' said Wilf.

'No,' I said, listening hard. 'She's going to kill Dad.'

We left them to it. They were clearly starting a particularly robust row, which, by the sound of it, was going to run and run. We wanted to investigate the rest of the flat.

Wilf opened a door at random. He stood, stunned, at the door, so I had to peer past him to see inside.

'This must be the bathroom,' I said after a long silence.

Wilf tiptoed into the huge room. Like the rest of the flat, the ceiling in there was very high. It boasted a flourishing array of cobwebs, and I swear there were eyes up there.

'Look at that bath,' said Wilf in a kind of awed whisper.

No question about it. 'British Museum,' I said. 'Egyptian. Sarcophagus, tenth dynasty. With taps, for the convenience of any resident body.'

'You could swim in the basin,' said Wilf, looking over the edge.

I took a quick peek. 'Don't think you'd want to. And I don't like the look of this loo.'

'Open the lid,' said Wilf. 'Go on, dare you.'

'It's got frogs carved on it.' I don't much like frogs.

'I don't think they are frogs,' said Wilf, after closer inspection.

I lifted the lid, kind of watchful. Then, slam!

'Why did you do that?'

I pointed dramatically at the lid. 'There's a face in there. With eyes. Looking straight at me.'

'Unlikely,' said Wilf.

And then, 'Eek! You're right.'

He lifted the lid again, very warily, and bravely took another look. 'It's all right, Beanbag. It's Napoleon.'

'What do you mean, it's all right? What's Napoleon doing in the loo?'

'It's a painting of his face. They used to have these in England. So when you go to the loo, you do it on his face.'

'That isn't very nice.'

'His enemies didn't think Napoleon was very nice.'

'How do you flush it? There's no cistern.'

'There is,' said Wilf, pointing up towards the ceiling. A heavy black metal tank was perched on two curly brackets.

I craned my neck, squinting up at it. 'What does it say on it?'

'Snood Sanitaryware, 1909,' said Wilf. 'And I suppose you flush it by pulling this.'

He gave the heavy chain a good tug. It had a handle charmingly shaped like a pineapple, which dug into his hand.

All hell broke loose.

First there was a heavy clunk.

Then a series of thuds and bangs from the cistern.

Then a few hideous squeals and squeaks.

And then what sounded like Niagara Falls, as the water surged into the bowl with such force that it made the lid rattle.

Wilf and I broke the world record for the backwards hop.

'And the moral of that is, don't flush the loo with the lid open.'

'And run as soon as you've pulled the chain.'

After what we'd seen so far the bedrooms, full of more darkly carved furniture and gloomy hangings, came as no surprise.

I bounced up and down on the mattress of a bed which was way off the floor.

'Don't do that,' said Wilf. 'Look at the dust.'

'This is great.'

Wilf wasn't committing himself. 'Depends on the music,' he said. 'But so far, so good.'

Five

THERE WAS ANOTHER ROW A FEW HOURS LATER, when Wilf and I were making plans for the next few days.

'We'll buy a street map and explore,' I said.

'Section it off,' suggested Wilf. 'Then do an area each day.'

'Sorry to disappoint you kids,' said Dad, still looking shell-shocked after the effort of cleaning the flat from top to bottom. As far as I could see, our combined efforts had made not the slightest difference to how it looked. Apart from anything else, I have my doubts about a cleaning cream labelled 'Blud – for every household purpose'.

'You're going to school tomorrow.'

Usually Dad couldn't put up with a joint onslaught of my firm statement of intentions, with the volume knob full on, and Wilf's relentless reasoning; but this time he was adamant.

'I've got to be at work first thing, and Mum isn't going to want you under her feet all day.'

'I certainly am not,' said Mum, her mind running on washing machines and fridges. 'Have you seen that antediluvian fridge in there? Noah must have kept his frozen chips in it.'

'It's a good size,' suggested Dad.

'Big enough for a body,' I said helpfully.

Dad rapidly changed the subject back to school. 'You're going, and that's that. They start early here, so you'd better get yourselves off to bed.'

Typical. Try another tack. 'We haven't had anything to eat.'

'How early is early?' asked Wilf.

'Finish up the odds and ends we brought in the cooler bag,' said Dad, getting up from the sofa with some difficulty. 'And school starts at eight.'

When the storm had subsided, and we finally had to concede defeat, we got down to the nitty gritty.

'What do we wear?'

'Who's going to drive us to school? You haven't got a car yet.'

'You wear your own clothes,' said Dad. 'We'll sort out any games kit you need later.'

'Great,' I said. 'Bet we'll stick out like a pair of sore thumbs.' I'm not wild about school uniform, but it has its advantages. Such as when you don't have a clue whether you wear jeans or trousers or a skirt. Your school bag is bound to be wrong as well. I had this feeling that at a new school in a very different country, everything about us was going to be a joke to the others.

Of course Wilf wasn't bothered. Wilf never wastes a single second worrying about what other people are doing or what they might be thinking of him. You have to admire him for this. It saves him no end of trouble.

'And you'll go to school on a tram. Number sixty-six stops just down the road, and drops you outside the gates of St Vlad's.'

'Tram?'

'St Vlad's? Are you serious?'

'I am. Vlad is a very popular name in this country. The present king is King Vlad. In fact, most of the kings they've had have been King Vlad. St Vlad was an ancestor of this present king.'

'Like St Edward,' said Wilf.

Dad's face showed that, from what he'd seen so far of Doume, he thought probably not at all like St Edward. He wasn't going to admit it, though. He concentrated on the box of cushions he was unpacking.

'Yes, that kind of thing,' he said. 'Now, get yourselves something to eat, and go to bed. Your mother needs time to recover.'

'Yes, like five years,' Wilf said as we chomped our way through some crisps and a bar or two of chocolate. It was rather a muted feast, I have to say. Mum is usually very good-tempered. She doesn't shriek and yell at us like some mothers I know; well, not often. Nothing much ruffles her, in the normal way. But she was ruffled now. First there was the argument with Dad, and there was no trace of a smile on her face as she watched me toying with a sad sandwich left over from lunch.

I didn't say much while we were eating. Don't get me wrong. I wasn't depressed, nothing like that, I'm not the depressive kind. But there are times when it's best to keep your head down, and this was one of them. I could see that Wilf was going to start again, as soon as he'd finished the last of the sausage rolls, so I kicked him under the table, very gently, just to give him a hint, and cast him a meaningful look.

'Why did you do that?' he asked when we'd got away. We'd hauled ourselves up on to my bed and were sitting with our feet dangling like some four-year-olds.

'Mum's in a mood.'

Wilf thought about that for a while. 'Yes, I suppose she is,' he said finally. Wilf doesn't much notice how other people are feeling, so you have to draw these things to his attention.

I said, 'Do you know what?'

Wilf didn't answer.

'Well? Don't you want to know what I'm going to say?'

'Not especially,' said Wilf. 'You're going to tell me whether I want to hear it or not.'

Having a forgiving nature, I ignored this remark. 'I think we're going to like it here,' I said.

Six

'FOUJAY WILL LOOK AFTER YOU, UM, BEATRICE.'

I had to put a stop to that before it began, although I also wanted to know who Foujay was. Foujay! What a name.

We were sitting in this high, dim room, which was the headmaster's office. It was panelled with dark wood, and the desk he was sitting behind was massive, with cunningly carved handles and pillars down the side.

'I'm usually called Beanbag,' I told the headmaster. Politely, but firmly.

He was a tall, lank man with a craggy face and crumpled dark hair. I could tell from his expression he wasn't too happy about calling me Beanbag.

'Don't like your own, um, name? You should get on splendidly with Foujay and his little friends, then.' He looked at Wilf. 'I have you down as Wilfred.'

Wilf shook his head. 'No thanks,' he said. 'Wilf.'

The headmaster sighed, and looked at his violin case. 'You must be musical,' he said in unenthusiastic tones.

There had been a scene over the violin that morning.

'Better not take it with you,' Mum had said brightly. 'It's quite valuable, and you can't be sure . . .'

'What Mum means is, it might be the kind of school where they'll take you apart if they see you with a violin.'

'It's possible, but unlikely,' said Wilf, after considering the matter.

You could see that Dad was longing to get going, but he wanted to hear Wilf's reasons.

'There's a lot in this place that's bizarre, right?' said Wilf, patiently.

'You could say that,' Dad said with feeling.

'So, since all these bizarre things don't bother them, why should a violin?'

Dad nodded. 'You may have a point there.'

I was getting impatient. 'Come on, Dad, he'll take it whatever you or Mum say.'

It was a bit mean of Dad just to dump us and run for it. Although you could tell that he'd been somewhat startled by the school when we got off the tram at the gates. 'Baroque,' he'd said in awed tones.

It actually looks like a very grand building with wrought iron everywhere in very strange curlicues and patterns.

'A far cry from your concrete-and-glass school back home,' Dad had said in a stunned voice. 'I'll just take you in, and then I must rush, I don't want to be late on my first day.'

'Aren't you going to tell the head all about us?'

'No.'

The headmaster gave another sigh as he flipped through Wilf's report. He sighs a lot. I think he has indigestion. 'It's clear that you're brainy,' he said to Wilf. 'What a nuisance.'

'Why are brains a nuisance?' asked Wilf.

'If you're bright, you'll already know the answer to that one. Take it from me, it's much easier to control a docile bunch of average, hard-working students. No anarchy, no original thinking, no questions. Brains and a violin don't bode well, I can tell you that.'

He swung round in his swivel chair. It had a wooden back which was decorated with more of those weird Doumian carvings like there were in our flat. His chair made groaning and howling noises as it turned. 'Ah, here's Foujay,' he said. 'This is, um, Beanbag. Joining us from, um , England. Look after her, will you?'

Foujay looked at me, and I looked at Foujay. My first impression was, this is one to watch. He's one of those wiry types, always on the move. He has wildly curly black hair and very dark eyes, and I thought right away he looked like a person who'd always have some scheme going.

'Okay, sir,' he said, looking at me in a fairly frosty way. 'This way, chummy.'

I hardly had time to tell Wilf that I'd see him at lunchtime before I found myself whirled along a dim corridor by this Foujay.

'Why Beanbag?' he said, sliding to a sudden halt. 'Let's get that straight first.'

I wasn't having any of it. 'Just because,' I said. 'Why Foujay?'

'It's my name. I appear on lists as Fouje, J. A. If you say it, it's Foujay. And don't ask me what the initials J. and A. stand for, because I won't tell you.'

'Thanks,' I said. I'd find out soon enough if I really wanted to know.

'You don't look like your brother,' remarked Foujay.

'So? I'm fair, and he's dark. He's musical, and I'm tone-deaf. He lives in a day dream, I'm practical. Want to make anything of it?'

'No,' said Foujay after a moment's thought. 'Not really.' We turned into yet another long and gloomy corridor.

'Nearly a mile of corridors here,' he said with satisfaction.

'Are they all as dark and sinister as these?'

'Worse,' said Foujay.

I couldn't believe what a horrible place it was. Although, actually, it's not bad once you get adjusted to it and think of it as a new reality.

We yomped along a few more miles of corridor, until Foujay skidded to a halt outside an enormous double door: carved as usual, and with a brass handle that looked as though it belonged in a castle.

'Our classroom,' he said, and made a rush at the door. I thought he'd fly in and across the room, but it barely opened a crack. Several more heaves opened it enough to go in.

When we made it inside, I wished we hadn't.

The classroom was amazing, and I just stood there in the doorway like a lemon. I expect my mouth was hanging open, too. It was like something out of an old film. Rows of desks, a blackboard, a teacher standing on a raised platform which ran across one end of the room . . .

I gaped, and the teacher gave me a fishy teacher's look, raised his eyebrows to the ceiling, pointed to an empty desk, and went on writing what looked like a lot of hieroglyphs on the board. I went where he'd pointed, and sat down. Nobody seemed very interested in me; back home, there would be a lot of whispering and staring if someone new suddenly joined the class.

I squinted hard at the board, and realized that the hieroglyphs were figures and letters, the kind of thing you see sixth-formers coping with. It boded ill, so I looked around me. The class was huge, about thirty-seven.

Let me tell you something else about classrooms at St Vlad's. They have nothing up on the walls. No samples of work to impress visitors or parents – well, that would be a waste of time. If anyone ever reached as far as our classroom they'd be in a state of exhaustion and in need of counselling.

No maps, no charts, no diagrams of the life cycle of the snail, no posters telling the pupils to do this or that. Just high, pointy windows, a lot more dark wood, and a ceiling which seemed to have three-D paintings on it.

On closer inspection, they weren't paintings at all. They were sculptures. Figures, mostly with no clothes on, dangling their feet down through a central dome.

I sat where I'd been told, which was next to Foujay. He saw me staring up at the ceiling.

'This used to be a royal palace,' he whispered.

'Ah,' I said. And then, 'What subject is this?'

'Maths,' said Foujay.

Oops. This was going to be worse than I'd feared. Much worse.

Seven

B EFORE I CAME TO DOUME, I NEVER THOUGHT
about doorbells. Doorbells are simple affairs. Little
white buttons in plastic surrounds. Press the button, and
a battery-operated bell rings. Or buzzes. Or, if you've
got a fancy one, plays a tune.

The one outside our apartment in Dread Street
doesn't belong to this class of doorbells. It's quite grand
to look at, with a brass surround, and a big white bit in
the middle, which tells you to Push. So far, not so
different. But does this connect to a battery and a silvery
tone inside?

It does not. When you press the bell, a wire is pulled
inside. At the end of the wire is a spiral of flat metal,
quite tightly wound. At the other end of the spiral is a
bell. A real ding-dong affair, with a clapper inside, like a
mini church bell.

Only not so mini as to give a gentle peal. Not at all. It
is a loud bell, and once set in motion, there is no way of
stopping its clamour until all the energy has gone from
the coil.

I rang it as gently as I could, after all, I was in shock. It
made no difference; I could see Mum's head reeling as
she dragged the door open for me. She was rubbing her
arm; our front door is very heavy, and would rather be
shut than open.

'Hello,' she said. 'Have you had a good day?' And, anxiously, 'Where's Wilf?'

I gave her a look. 'Wilf won't be back till late.'

'Why not?'

I put my bag down on the marble floor. 'He's singing. He's joined the choir, and they practise until five. He's also in the orchestra, and they rehearse after that.'

Mum's jaw dropped. 'It's his first day.'

'So? When has that ever made any difference to Wilf?' I collapsed into the sofa. 'Is there anything to eat? They have the strangest food in the cafeteria. Hot peppers in everything, and very peculiar vegetables.'

'You'd better take a packed lunch tomorrow. Come into the kitchen and tell me all about your day.'

She'd been shopping, and handed me a crusty bread roll. It didn't look edible, but I was past caring. Surprise, surprise, it was good. 'What are the black bits on top?' I asked. 'Fly droppings?'

'Poppy seed.'

I wasn't too sure about that, but I finished it up anyway.

'So, have you made any friends?'

I decided to tell the truth. 'Nope. I've been carted about from pillar to post by this guy that the head told to look after me. He's called Foujay, but we won't go into why he's called that. He's got a cousin in the school that he goes around with. A real dumbo, but quite nice, and he's called Hardhat.'

'Hardhat?'

'He was sent a helmet from America, because he's always falling off his roller skates and having iron girders fall on his head and things like that. He's very big and burly. But, like I said, dense. I'll probably find myself sitting next to him in maths tomorrow,' I added. 'Seeing

— 28 —

that they're bound to shove me down into the bottom maths group.'

Mum made soothing noises. 'Has Wilf made any friends?'

'Apart from the choir, everyone who plays in the orchestra, the maths teacher, the dinner lady who ladles out the potatoes and the school cat? Which, incidentally, has fangs.'

'You're being unfair.'

'On the cat?'

'On Wilf.'

'I'm not. That boy is a serious embarrassment, you have to believe me.'

I heaved myself up from the sofa.

'Lots of homework?' enquired Mum, in her interested-parent voice.

'Things to bone up on. Where's that guidebook?'

I retreated to my room and opened the long, tall window as wide as it would go, to let in more light. Then I settled down on the bed, with an apple I'd taken from the bowl as I went past. I was going to get to grips with *The Darkside Guide to the Kingdom of Doume*.

There was a lot about this country I felt I needed to know.

THE DARKSIDE GUIDE TO
THE KINGDOM OF DOUME

The three principal buildings in Valderk are the Castle Bane, the New Palace and the Town Hall.

TOWN HALL

The Town Hall dates from the sixteenth century, and is heavily fortified. It is built in granite, and its massive gateway took fifty years to complete. Master Osric designed the gateway and its fine carvings before going mad in 1573 when he was confined to the Monastery of St Vlad.

Within the gateway, the visitor comes to a central courtyard. Many doors lead off it, and there are several stairways leading up to the first floor and to the gallery on the second floor.

The tourist office is situated somewhere on the ground floor, but since none of the doors is labelled and the office is regularly moved, it is difficult to obtain any information about anything.

NEW PALACE

The New Palace looks like a Town Hall. It was constructed in the nineteenth century by King Vlad the Grab, who confiscated lots of properties, sold them, and built himself a new palace with the proceeds. There are three hundred and sixty-five rooms in the palace, a network of dungeons in the basement, and, at the last count, seventy-two turrets. The New Palace is now the home of the Museum of Doumian Armour and Decorative Arts and houses the National Art Collection.

CASTLE BANE

Castle Bane is the official residence of the present king and his family. It is situated on the western side of Valderk and spreads over most of a rocky peak overlooking the capital. The castle was built in the fourteenth century to repel marauding Hungarians; it is in the style known as Doumian Grim Romanesque.

The Royal Standard flies above the central tower of Castle Bane when the present King, Vlad XXIII (known as Comrade Vlad), is in residence. It is easily recognizable, being quartered with the royal symbols of the Magpie of Doume, couchant; a Double-headed Bat, pendant; a Fanged Cat, rampant; and the Great Horn of Doume, muted, all against a red background.

Eight

FOUJAY, OF COURSE, KNEW BETTER. I TOOK THE *Darkside* book into school with me the next day, and he was very sniffy about it, flipping through the pages and pointing out all the mistakes.

'It's all wrong, what it says here about the castle flag,' he said, pointing to the page. 'It hangs there all the time whether old Vlad's in or not, because the rope's all knotted up. So they can't haul it down. I don't know why you bought this book, it's a load of nonsense.'

'It belongs to my parents, and it's very useful and informative.'

'Have you read all those pages?' said Hardhat, with respect, as he tried to heave his skateboard up the step and instead landed with a crash against the wall.

'If you didn't run into things all the time, you'd be able to read,' I said, wincing at the sound of the impact.

Hardhat thought about that for a bit, and then he shook his head. 'No, I don't think so,' he said. 'My pa's not very bright, and he doesn't run into things.'

'Your dad's not been very bright since he was dropped on his head by a Russian wrestler in the Olympics,' said Foujay.

I was impressed. 'Your dad was in the Olympics?'

'Yes,' said Hardhat.

Foujay was drumming his fingers against the wall. He hated to be still. 'Anyone can get to the Olympics from

— 32 —

Doume. Wrestling, fencing and archery. That's what we're good at.'

'I've never seen anyone from Doume win a medal.'

'Oh, we never win any medals. I said we get to compete, because they let little countries like us in for the spectators to ooh and aah at when they watch the opening shindig.'

'So Doumians aren't actually any good at those sports?'

'We are, in fact, very good. We just don't have the same rules as other countries. Our rules are much more interesting, but it means we get disqualified.'

'So how come Hardhat's dad got dropped on his head? If you're so good?'

'You should see the Russian.'

'I haven't got to sport yet,' I said, snatching the guidebook back.

'You don't want to bother with that,' said Foujay. 'I know much more about the Kingdom of Doume than any old book.'

'Thank you, but I prefer to read the book.'

Foujay shrugged. 'Suit yourself. Want a Zizzo?'

I love Zizzo, but I was feeling narky. 'Oh, can you get Zizzo here? How surprising.'

Foujay looked at me as though I was bonkers. 'Course you can. We make it.'

'Under licence, I suppose. Zizzo's an American drink. Everyone knows that.'

'Then everyone knows wrong. True, it's *sold* in America; it's sold all over the world. But it comes from Doume. We've got a special formula, nobody knows what goes into it. And it's Zizzo that keeps Doume going, because people love it, and the more we make, the more they drink. If it weren't for Zizzo, Doume would be bankrupt. Wiped out.'

Hardhat took a quick swig of Foujay's Zizzo and then executed a particularly spectacular jump and twist, and then landed without falling over or running into anything. 'Olé,' he said triumphantly. 'That's what Zizzo does for you.'

It's funny, isn't it, how when something's cropped up once, it does it again.

It was like that with Zizzo. And to say it's a coincidence isn't really accurate, because Zizzo just took over our lives. The whole thing really began that afternoon when I drank all of Foujay's bottle, which didn't please him very much.

Then, when I got home – guess what, Wilf was doing music after school again – Mum whipped into the kitchen and came out with a can of chilled Zizzo. I didn't mention that I'd already had one at school, because Mum gets fussy about teeth and too many fizzy drinks.

'Did you know Zizzo comes from Doume?'

Mum did. She'd been making some enquiries about work, it turned out. She's a graphic designer, and has dreamed up a lot of labels in her time. The mention of work was a bit worrying, though. It made it seem as though we were going to stay in Doume for longer than a just a little while.

'It's going to be a busy time for your father,' she said. 'It's a bigger job than he'd realised.'

'Oh?'

'A lot of treasures have been stolen. One or two have been found, but most of the others have vanished. They haven't turned up for sale anywhere.'

Like I said, Dad's area of expertise is museums, libraries, art galleries and so on. You wouldn't believe what gets lifted from these places. Huge chunks of marble, vast paintings, great heavy chunks of bronze. Sometimes the crooks just wheel the stuff out, it's astonishing how short-sighted some of these museum staff are. Still, I'd lose my own marbles if I had to sit on a chair watching people looking at Egyptian mummies or Neolithic pots all day long. It must addle their brains.

The Zizzo got to me, and I burped, much to Mum's disapproval. To distract her, I asked some more questions about these thefts. 'A spate, is it?'

'A what?'

'It's what they call it in the papers. A spate of burglaries.'

'Oh, I see. Yes, I suppose you could call it a spate. Ask your father, it's not secret. Most of the thefts and break-ins have been reported in the papers here. Anybody can read about them.'

Anybody meant me. 'Have we got any of the papers?'

'There's a file of cuttings on the desk,' said Mum. 'It's good for business, all these break-ins, because now they've decided they want Dad to help them track down the culprit as well as advising about how to make sure nothing else gets pinched.'

Dad usually gets called in to shut the stable door after the proverbial horse has bolted. The bigwigs all sit around wringing their hands and asking how it could have happened, and then they'll pay anything to make sure it doesn't happen again. But Dad doesn't usually have much to do with haring after the criminals.

'They think it's an international art thief,' said Mum, who had been shuffling through papers on the desk and now handed me a fat pink file with an elastic band round it. 'They hope your father will understand his mind and give them valuable hints and tips about his psychology.'

I made a disbelieving noise and retreated to my room, clutching the pink file and ignoring the cries of 'Homework?' which wafted after me.

Parents have no sense of priorities.

There was the stuff about the Hand of Doume from the Cathedral. Then there was the disappearance of the Golden Cup of Doume, the daytime removal of the painting of the Martyrdom of St Vlad the Good and the lost carvings from the King's Palace. I read, too, about the very strange theft of the Craque of Doume from the Monastery of St Vlad the Good.

The Daily Doume

Crime Wave of art thefts

In recent weeks, several fine works of art have been stolen from galleries, museums and other collections. In addition to the curious case of the disappearance of the Hand of Doume the nation has suffered the loss of a great painting, the Martyrdom of St Vlad, from the Municipal Art Gallery. Several irreplaceable ancient volumes from the Academy, written in Doumian, have vanished. Carvings have beed lifted from the panelled Great Chamber of the King's Palace. And the Golden Bowl of Doume, a priceless mediaeval cup, was stolen from the Valderk Museum.

There are many theories about the crimes.

It is suggested that the works of art are going to be held to ransom. This would be foolish, as there is no money to pay any ransom, as any Doumian with half his or her wits knows perfectly well. Supporters of this theory maintain that this proves the crimes to be the work of foreigners, unaware of the emptiness of the Doumian purse.

Another theory put forward is that the crimes have been committed by one or more of the Undead, determined to get their revenge on the living. We ask, why should they? We Doumians don't bother the Undead, and they only occasionally bother us.

Then there is the idea that these works have been targeted for theft by people working on behalf of mad collectors. Investigator Drinkwater dismisses this notion, saying that no collector would be mad enough to want some of these Doumian items. We have to agree.

The most likely explanation is a gang of international art thieves, planning to stash the items away until they are no longer 'hot', and then sell them, perhaps altered in some way, or melted down if gold, to fences in the Underworld. Doume, as we all know, has a widespread and wicked Underworld.

Nine

I WANTED TO ASK DAD A FEW QUESTIONS ABOUT ALL these weird crimes, but I didn't get the chance.

None of us had got used to the phone yet. It was a big, old-fashioned affair, with yards of tightly curled wire attached to a squat black base with a luminous dial. On top was a large, heavy receiver. It was the sort of phone you see in old black-and-white movies.

'No danger of big phone bills here,' said Dad. 'You'd get a numb arm if you tried to hold this thing for more than a minute or so.'

The really awful thing about the phone is the sound it makes. It wails. It goes: "Eeeeeeooouuuuuieee.' The first time it rang Dad dropped several plates in the kitchen. Mum wrapped a towel round the bell in the hall – a big towel, because it was a big bell – but, if anything, it sounded even more sinister when muffled.

I was sitting at the big black table, having finally got down to my homework, and I made a great blob with my pen on the page when the banshee shriek went off.

'Phone!' yelled Mum from the bathroom.

'I *know*,' I shouted, picking up the receiver with both hands. 'Hello?'

It was Dad, to say Something Had Come Up, and he wouldn't be back until very late indeed.

'What's happened?' I asked. I am by nature curious, and I've noticed that if you just ask straight out, often as not people will tell you. Not this time; the line had gone dead. I didn't know if Dad would have said more or not; it sounded as though we'd been cut off. He probably wouldn't have told me, in any case. Apart from knowing when to keep his mouth shut, he's careful about what he says on the phone. Dad's suspicious about phones – all phones. 'Too easy to tamper with, or listen in to,' he says. He's very security-minded, of course, it goes with the job.

In fact, I didn't need to interrogate Dad. When I got to school the next day, it turned out that Foujay knew all about why Dad had stayed late at work. I sometimes think Foujay knows too much about everything.

'Hot news,' he said, perching himself beside me on the wall where I was peacefully attacking my lunch box. I hadn't seen him that morning; we were in different sets for a lot of subjects.

'Oh?' I said, trying not to sound interested.

'Your dad's involved,' he went on, unwrapping his sandwiches.

'Oh?' I said again. And then, alarmed, 'Watch out, here comes Hardhat.'

Hardhat whizzed round the corner, missed us by a whisker, and went full tilt into the grass bank on the other side of the path.

'Good thing that wasn't the wall,' he said, picking himself up. 'I reckon this skateboard's got something wrong with it, it won't go anywhere I want.'

He hauled a mangled roll out of his pocket. 'I think I landed on my lunch,' he said. 'Has Foujay told you the big news?'

'I'm trying to,' said Foujay, quite snappy for him. 'Now, listen. You remember I told you that Zizzo is made in Doume?'

'Yes. So what, that isn't news.'

'Zizzo is made to a secret formula.'

'And?'

'It's a formula handed down from centuries ago. It needs a very special combination of rare-plant extracts, that's what gives it that tangy taste. The monks out at the monastery concocted the drink centuries ago, liked it a lot, and wrote the recipe down. They kept it on the altar, in a box, along with St Vlad the Good's finger. Then some local nob came along and threatened to throw the monks out. They gave him the formula as a bribe so that they could stay.'

'I thought they did get chucked out,' said Hardhat. You could tell he was concentrating, because he was cracking his knuckles.

Foujay wasn't very interested in the monks, he wanted to tell me about the formula. 'Do stop that, Hardhat. But you're right; the nob grabbed the formula, and then booted the monks out anyway.'

Hardhat shook his head, and made an indrawn whistling noise. 'Doesn't do to treat monks like that. You never know what they might do in revenge.'

Crack, crack.

'A few of them gradually drifted back to the monastery and it started up again. What's important is that the formula for Zizzo didn't go back to the monks, it was kept by the local family who'd nicked it. They made gallons of it at the harvest and other festivals. Then times got hard. The grandson of the man who got his hands on the formula was a gambler and he lost all his money.'

'So I suppose he sold the formula,' I said. Who would have thought a fizzy drink would have its own personal history?

'Wrong,' said Foujay. 'He had a daughter, who was

one tough cookie. She saw the potential of Zizzo, and started the business in order to restore the family fortunes. That was about a hundred years ago.'

'Hey, is Zizzo that old?' Hardhat crammed the remains of his roll into his mouth and got to his feet. He did a few swoops to show his interest. 'I thought it had only been going for a few years before the commies took over.'

'Commies?'

'You haven't read that rubbishy guidebook properly, have you?' said Foujay smugly. 'Doume was communist until a few years back, when the Berlin Wall came down, and hard-line lefties went out of fashion. Mind you,' he added, 'I can't say they were ever exactly in fashion here in Doume, but we weren't given the choice.'

'You've got a king,' I said. Even I know that communist states bump off any kings and so forth who are unwise enough to be hanging around come the revolution. It's usually the first thing they do; we'd covered it in history under Revolutions and Rebellions.

'He's been restored,' said Foujay impatiently. 'Never mind about him, you can read it up later. It's got nothing to do with Zizzo. Now, Zizzo wasn't allowed when the communists were running the country. They said that was a decadent capitalist drink. Fizzy meant Western, so Zizzo was banned.' He polished an apple on his sleeve. 'But actually, as everybody knows, they banned it because they couldn't make it.'

'Why couldn't they make it?'

'Zora, who was the great-granddaughter of the woman who founded the Zizzo company, escaped from Doume with the secret formula.'

'And made Zizzo somewhere else?'

Foujay shook his head. 'No way. The secret ingredients are plants and herbs which you only find in Doume.

Until now. I mean, nowadays, if you had the formula, you could copy the plant extracts chemically.'

'Where's the formula now? Is Zora in Doume now?'

'Yes. She came tripping back to start up the factories again as soon as the communists fell and there was a new government.'

'Only now the formula's been stolen.'

'It would be worth a fortune to a company in another country, and if they can make Zizzo somewhere else, outside Doume, then the Doumian economy will collapse.'

'Doume and gloom' I said.

Foujay glared at me. 'Very funny.'

'Sorry. Hang on, though. Zizzo's made all over the place. There's a big Zizzo plant outside Birmingham, you can see it from the train.'

'Yup,' said Foujay. 'But they get the master concentrate from Doume. It's made here, once a year. They take the formula to the monastery, the monks gather this and that, one plant each, so none of them knows the complete recipe. Then it gets shipped out all over the world to the Zizzo bottling plants.'

'And this formula's been stolen?'

'Yes.'

'How do you know?'

'Lulu told me.'

Ten

'LULU?' WHO ON EARTH WAS LULU? AND HOW would she know what my father was doing?

'His aunt,' shouted Hardhat as he rattled past. 'Foujay's mum's sister.'

Hardhat did some of his more of his life-threatening jumps, thundering up the bank and turning a somersault.

'He makes me feel seasick,' I said. 'What about this Lulu? What does she have to do with the Zizzo formula?'

'She's Stuka's girlfriend,' said Foujay.

Stuka. Stuka? The name rang a bell, but I was so wrapped up in the Zizzo story that I couldn't make the connection. There was a terrific clatter as Hardhat made a violent sudden turn and sent the wheel spinning off his skateboard. He picked himself up and looked at his damaged board with awe. 'Just Stuka's name is enough to do damage,' he said.

'Stuka's the Head of the Secret Police,' said Foujay. 'Everyone knows that.'

'I don't. Why should I?'

'He's world-famous,' said Foujay. 'His picture's always in the papers.'

That was it. Stuka was in all those items about the Crime Wave of Doume. The Spate.

Foujay could tell I wasn't that impressed. 'Take it

from me, Stuka is one big cheese, and he knows everything. The formula's gone missing, Stuka will be kept informed. Of course, he isn't supposed to be involved with mere everyday criminals, not being in charge of the Civil Police. That's Rudi's job.'

'Rudi?'

'Rudi Drinkwater, Chief Cop. Head of Criminal Investigation.'

I'd heard the name. He was the one who'd brought my father over from England.

'Poor Rudi, he can count on Stuka poking his nose in, especially if it's going to get into the papers. Stuka loves having his picture in the papers.'

I'm not really up on Intelligence and Spies, but I thought the whole point was secrecy. A publicity-hungry Chief of Secret Police seemed unlikely. 'And he tells this Lulu person, your aunt, what's going on?'

'Yup. She's very nosy, likes to know what's going on.'

'Very bad security,' I said.

'Lulu's quite discreet, when she wants to be,' said Foujay.

Hardhat nodded. 'Better than Stuka's wife,' he said. 'She always blabbed everything she knew.'

'What's happened to the wife?' I asked, my mind turning to dungeons.

'They went on a trip to London, and he lost her in Harrods.'

'Lost her?'

'Mmm. Hasn't seen her since.'

'He gets the bills, though,' put in Hardhat, rubbing his knees. 'From Harrods. So she's probably still there.'

Wilf came round the corner, violin case in one hand, a bottle of Zizzo in the other. I was, for once, glad to see him. With all his faults, Wilf has a good brain. He'd make sense of this Zizzo business.

'Listen,' I said. 'Foujay, you tell about Zizzo, and how it got made.'

'No need to do that,' said Wilf, hitching himself on to the wall and putting his violin carefully down beside him. 'We did it in Food Technology yesterday. Quite interesting; beats making veggie soup, anyhow. So what about Zizzo?'

'Tell him about Lulu,' I said.

'Stuka's mistress,' Wilf said at once.

You can see why my brother's fairly difficult to live with.

'All right, know-all,' I said. 'Now for something you don't know. The formula's been stolen.'

Wilf thought for a moment about that, then shrugged his shoulders. 'So? Must be plenty of the mixture around. And they must know how to make more, surely it's written down at headquarters. Or probably kept on computer, these days.'

'No,' said Foujay. 'It isn't. And I reckon whoever's taken it is going to sell it to the highest bidder, and that won't be anyone in Doume. He'll take it abroad.'

'When did it go missing?' asked Wilf.

'They discovered it had gone yesterday,' said Hard-hat, managing, for once, to stop short of the wall. 'That's what Lulu said. She won't say any more, though. Except that whoever took the formula left a message in its place.'

'Message?'

'Yes, a piece of curled-up paper which looked just like the formula.'

'Only it wasn't?'

'No. It just said, in big letters, "Ha, ha".'

★

Dad staggered into the apartment, exhausted, at about half past ten that evening, rubbing his arm from where the door had had a go at him. It was Friday night, and Wilf and I were still up, waiting for him.

Wilf grabbed his briefcase and pushed him into an armchair. I whisked into the kitchen and rushed back with a tall glass of ice-cold beer.

Silence, except for glugging noises.

I fetched him another cold beer. Mum was in the kitchen, muttering and grumbling as she heaved open the oven door to put Dad's meal in.

'Stone cold,' she said furiously. 'What kind of a time is this?'

'He's often home late.'

'Yes, but he lets me know. Or I can phone him at work. Try that here and they say there's a cordon of security and nobody can speak to anybody. I never heard such nonsense.'

I could see that she was going to surge into the sitting room and let fly at Dad. That would put him in a really bad mood, and he wouldn't tell us anything. 'It's not his fault,' I said in cheery tones. 'They work differently here.'

'They do everything differently here,' she said through gritted teeth.

'It's all experience, that's what you said to us.'

'Never mind what I said to you.'

She was starting to simmer down; thank goodness.

'I'll make you a cup of tea,' I offered.

Mum gave me that look which mothers all have for when they don't trust you an inch. 'Go on,' she said. 'Spit it out.'

'It's just that Wilf and I are a bit interested in this case Dad's working on.'

'Hence the beer and the buttering up.'

'Exactly.'

She sighed. 'I'm going back to my room to finish some letters I'm writing. Keep an eye on the oven, and give him his food when it's ready. There's some salad in the fridge. Now, I don't want to be disturbed for at least an hour.'

Phew. That was lucky.

Restored by the beer and the good smells coming out of the kitchen, Dad was surprisingly willing to spill the beans. 'It's not a situation I like,' he told us. 'I was employed by Drinkwater strictly as a security adviser, to make sure Doumian museums and galleries and all the other buildings with valuable collections are properly protected. End of brief. But this Stuka guy, who carries a lot of clout, has hauled me on to the investigation side.' He pulled at his tie and took off his jacket. 'Phew, that's better. Anyway, I don't like it, and I can see that Rudi D. doesn't like it, either. Well, you can hardly blame him, can you? He doesn't believe it's an international crook who's behind this. He says they're local crimes, committed by local people. And I'm inclined to agree with him.'

Usually Dad's downright cagey as can be when he's on a case, but he needed to get that off his chest, and, as he said, most of it would be all over the papers the next day.

It was.

VITAL ZIZZO FORMULA STOLEN

Crime waves rises to new heights as formula vanishes – Government in chaos

King pleads for calm

Zizzo shares crash on Valderk exchange – Wall Street shudders

US president offers financial aid and troops

European Union says it is watching the situation closely

Zizzo gone:
is Doume doomed?

Stuka stuck!

Zizzo zizzed – what now for Doume?

Cola shares soar worldwide

Eleven

I'D NIPPED OUT EARLY TO GET THE PAPER FROM THE crone who sold it on the corner of our street.

'Trouble for your dad,' she said with a knowing wink. 'Oh, dearie me, yes.'

'How do these people know so much?' said Dad, looking much better after a night's sleep. He took one look at the headlines blazing out from the papers, and groaned. 'That man Stuka's a complete maniac. I've never worked with anyone like him in my life.'

'It's all rubbish,' he went on, thumping one of the papers which lay open on the table. He bit savagely into a piece of toast. 'There are fingerprints. They're the same fingerprints as have been found at the scene of other crimes. They don't belong to any of the suspects in any of the cases.'

Wilf was reading more on the inside pages. 'It's says they've arrested an Englishman, and there's a picture of him on page five. Do you know him, Dad?'

I looked over his shoulder. It wasn't a good picture, more one of the figure-in-a-fog kind, but he looked familiar. 'I do. It's the man we met at the airport. Mr Johnson.'

Dad winced. 'Yes, it's Johnson, and his arrest will cause a big flap. He's only half English, and that half is related to the Ambassador and goodness knows who else, and on the Doume side he's a cousin of King Vlad.'

I was impressed.

'Don't be,' said Dad. 'The present king's grandfather, Vlad the Bad, spread himself around a bit; there are hundreds of cousins. But it doesn't help.'

'Did he take it?'

Dad shrugged. 'Maybe. He's a natural suspect, he's in the business, knows how valuable the formula is . . . It's all too obvious, though. And he didn't have access to the key to the safe. He's a non-starter as a suspect.'

'Key?' asked Foujay, interested, when we reported our findings to him. 'Wasn't the safe broken into?'

'No, it was locked and the combination properly set; Dad was definite about that.'

At least there was something Foujay's auntie Lulu hadn't known. Foujay tends to know everything. It can be very annoying, when his black eyes sparkle and he comes out with some fact before you've had a chance to mention it. I like to be first with the news, well, who doesn't, and Foujay was too often there in front of me as far as this affair was concerned. Still, it put me on my mettle, which is where you need to be when you're dealing with Doume and Doumians.

'I don't suppose Stuka noticed,' said Foujay. 'He's like a bull in a china shop, is Stuka. He arrests everyone at the scene of crime first, and settles the details afterwards.'

'Very sloppy,' said Wilf disapprovingly. 'How does he get away with it?'

'It isn't good police procedure,' agreed Foujay. 'But at least they're only arrested. Under the last regime they arrested them just the same, only they sent them all off to the salt mines.'

'Ah,' I said, feeling rather out of my depth.

We had joined up with Foujay at a café round the

corner from our apartment. It was called the Nix café, and it was a busy place. It was also quite unlike any café I'd ever been in.

It wasn't just the dark paint, deep red and black and purple.

Or the guttering torches burning in huge metal sconces on the walls.

Or the black marble tables.

Or the people, who seemed like a whole new race of beings. Aliens, in fact.

It was the whole atmosphere. I liked the Nix. I liked it a lot. That's the thing about living in Doume: you never know what you're going to come across next. It keeps you on your toes, and means that life's never dull. Anyway, if the Nix is what being part of café society is all about, then I'm all for it.

'Strange types in here,' said Wilf, who didn't usually pay much attention to his surroundings or to other people.

'They're students,' said Foujay. 'The university's near here.'

'Do all the students look like this lot?' I asked.

Foujay gave a great grin, and laughed. 'You mean the gaunt look?'

'And the jet-black hair and dead-white faces and red lipstick.'

'That's only the boys,' added Wilf. 'Look at the girls.'

I preferred not to.

'It's the fashion,' said Foujay. 'My sister's a student, so I'm used to it.'

That was all right, then.

Something had been puzzling Wilf. He has an orderly mind, and likes to get everything clear.

'Stuka's the head of the Secret Police, is that right?'

'Yes,' said Foujay. 'SKULK, they're called.'

'Then what's he got to do with all this? Isn't it up to the ordinary police to solve a crime where something's been stolen?'

'It is and it isn't,' said Foujay. 'Look at it like this. One, as I told you when the story broke, Stuka loves to see his picture in the paper. As often as possible. Important crimes are newsworthy, so he muscles in. Two, the head of the Civil Police, our Rudi, is too clever by half, in Stuka's view. He trained in America, so he knows all about modern policing.'

'Then surely he's the guy who should be in charge on this job.'

'No, no,' said Foujay. 'Modern policing is very un-Doumian. Very suspect.'

Wilf didn't look convinced.

'Three, Stuka hates Rudi's guts.'

Foujay pulled down his third finger. 'Four, Zizzo's a national asset. Therefore, it's a state matter, therefore Stuka's taken over command.'

I wondered how Rudi felt about all this, but Foujay said airily that he probably didn't really mind, he was a retiring sort of character, tall and thin and no person-ality.

'Stuka, on the other hand, makes quite an impression. He's tall and chunky and sinister.'

I could see that this was a minefield. Poor Dad, come out to advise on security, and he gets caught up in all this.

The door of the café swung open, and Hardhat careered through the entrance, sending a waitress flying, and wrapping himself round a barleycorn pillar which supported the gallery upstairs.

'No blades in here,' bellowed a large man from behind the bar.

'Where's your skateboard?' I asked, as we helped him undo his boots.

'Roller skates are faster,' he said, slumping into a chair. 'There's news. About the missing formula case.'

'What news?' asked Foujay, all alert.

'My dad's been arrested.'

Twelve

WILF AND I STARED AT HARDHAT.
'That's awful,' I said.

'What have they arrested him *for*?' asked Wilf.

'Stealing the secret Zizzo formula,' said Hardhat.

'Sit down,' said Foujay.

Hardhat did so, clanking his blades against the metal support of the table, shaking everything on it and adding to the other sounds which poured out of the Nix. 'That's really stupid,' said Foujay, once Hardhat was settled. 'Why should your dad steal the secret formula?'

Hardhat was trying to look as though he didn't mind about his father, but I'm sure he did. Although his expression never varied much, I knew there was a worried look in his eyes. I asked him if he wanted a Zizzo, and then could have kicked myself for being so tactless.

'No, I do not want a Zizzo,' said Hardhat firmly. 'I'll have a blood-and-bones, please.'

Wilf and I looked at each other. 'Blood-and-bones?'

'It's a kind of sundae, with ice cream and meringue and raspberry juice,' said Hardhat. 'I'm very hot.'

'You must be very worried about your dad. Shouldn't you be at home?'

'Oh, no,' said Hardhat, who was beginning to sound and look more cheerful. 'You see, Dad's always getting arrested.'

Foujay edged his way back through the throng with a tall glass in one hand and a long spoon in the other. He dumped it in front of Hardhat, grabbed his chair back from a passing student who was trying to make off with it, and took a good drink of his Zizzo.

'What's that black blob in there, Hardhat?' I didn't like the look of it at all.

'Ice cream,' said Hardhat, taking a hefty mouthful.

Ugh.

Wilf was keeping his mind on the matter in hand. 'Hardhat says his dad's always getting arrested.'

'He is,' said Hardhat indistinctly.

'Yes, I know,' said Foujay. 'But this is different, Hardhat. Smuggling salami across the border is one thing, stealing the most valuable thing in Doume is another. The whole country depends on Zizzo. If Zizzo goes, everyone will have to get a proper job.'

Salami? Whoever heard of anyone smuggling salami? Just when you think you're getting to grips with this place, along comes something like salami-smuggling. I ask you.

'Hardhat's dad and his uncle have got a good wheeze going,' said Foujay. 'We make very good salami in Doume, and it's a lot cheaper than across the border. So they slap a thumping great tax on it over there, to stop our stuff wiping theirs out in the shops. Hardhat's uncle lives up at the edge of the Forest of Gloom, so he does regular runs to the other side. Hardhat's father buys the salami from a friend in Valderk.'

'The local police know all about it,' said Hardhat, chasing a lump of ice cream round his glass. 'They get a cut, but they have to arrest someone from time to time, to show they're keen and stop anyone thinking they're corrupt.'

'But they are,' pointed out Wilf.

'There's corrupt and corrupt,' said Foujay quickly. 'Hardhat's dad and his uncle take it in turns to be arrested.' He frowned and shook his head. 'But why haul him in for this? You dad couldn't steal a bottle of milk out of a fridge, Hardhat, let alone open a safe and get away with a secret formula.'

'You said he wouldn't want to steal the formula,' I said.

'No, he wouldn't. That kind of thing is right outside his field. Besides, how would he know what he's taking? He sees letters back to front and upside down, can't read anything, can he, Hardhat?'

'No,' said Hardhat. 'But that wouldn't matter, not with that old formula.'

'What do you mean?'

'Well, nobody can read it, can they? That's why they showed it to us when we went round on that school trip. I mean, if anybody could read it, they wouldn't get it out and show it to us, would they?'

'You mean you didn't get to see it close up,' said Foujay. 'I didn't know you were short-sighted.'

Hardhat looked puzzled. 'Short-sighted? Why should I be short-sighted?'

'You were the one who said you couldn't read the secret formula.'

I had a brainwave. 'Hardhat, do you mean it was written in Latin, or some language like that?'

Hardhat looked doubtful. 'It could be. I don't know any Latin. Does it have funny letters?'

'That's Greek,' said Wilf.

'Why would the secret formula be in Greek?' I said.

'It isn't,' said Foujay. 'This is beginning to get interesting. Hardhat, why didn't you tell us you'd actually seen the formula?'

Hardhat thought about that for a while. 'Because you didn't ask.'

Foujay pulled his chair closer to the table and yanked a notebook out of his pocket. It was brand-new by the look of it, black and shiny, with strange patterns on it. He felt in his other pocket and drew out a fat fountain pen. 'I bought the notebook on my way here,' he said. 'I had a feeling we might need it.'

I thought he was going to get to the bottom of the strange script of the formula, but he said, no, no, he could guess what that was. 'Aren't you going to tell us?'

'No. Work it out for yourselves. It isn't important.'

That shows how wrong even someone as clued-up as Foujay can be.

Wilf liked the look of the notebook. 'I wouldn't mind one like that. What do you need it for?'

'Notes,' said Foujay. 'I'm going to be a detective when I finish my education. So this is good practice, follow the case, keep tabs on the expert.'

'What, on Stuka?'

'No, of course no. What does he do? Runs round in circles and arrests everybody in sight, including Hard-hat's dad.'

'When will Hardhat's dad be released? Does he get out on bail?'

Foujay thought about that. 'Depends if Stuka's serious about him or not. He'll probably just have to pay the usual bribe, only it's called a fine, and then he's free.'

'Fine? Bribe? What about being charged, magistrates, trial, even?'

'Not when it's a Secret Service arrest.' Foujay had produced a Biro, one of the Doumian specials, shaped like a flaming torch, and had written in large letters at the top of a blank page in his notebook: **The Zizzo Case.**

'When you're arrested by the Secret Police, you pay your fine and off you go.'

'What? No matter what you've done?'

'Oh, they never arrest anyone who's actually guilty of anything. They're usually behind the skulduggery, and they aren't going to arrest themselves, are they? No, the whole point is to arrest perfectly innocent people. That's how Stuka funds SKULK. Don't bother about Stuka. We're going to concentrate on Rudi Drinkwater. He knows what he's doing. He'll find out who's stolen the Zizzo formula, and we'll be shadowing him while he's on the case, learning all his tradecraft.'

'Eh?' said Hardhat, alarmed. He cracked a knuckle or two, and Foujay, as was his way, chewed a curl of hair which just reached his mouth.

'You'll get a hairball in your stomach, if you do that,' I told him.

Thirteen

I STUFFED FOUJAY'S NOTES INTO A POCKET AS WE
left the Nix. Hardhat had hurled himself off on his
blades, and Foujay was in a tearing hurry; he had been
due home half an hour ago. 'Got to visit an uncle,' he
said, running for a tram.

Wilf and I stood on the pavement, watching trams
and the erratic Doumian traffic flowing past. Horns
hooted, people waved and screeched at other drivers
through car windows; further along, by the out-of-order
traffic lights, a policeman was standing in a swirl of
angry vehicles, reading the lurid headlines in yesterday's
Shout.

'Shall we go for a mooch?' Wilf suggested.

With Foujay's revelations fresh in my mind, I felt we
ought to head for home, to get some more info out of
Dad.

'No point,' said Wilf. 'He was going into the office
until after lunch. We can pump him later on, he said
he'd take us to a film.'

Wilf was right, and, besides, we had our pocket
money and I fancied a stroll in the town centre.

'Tram?'

'Let's walk. We can buy chocolate with the fare
money.'

Wilf considered. 'Cheap chocolate or extremely good
chocolate?'

Cheap chocolate meant a slab from one of the newsagents-cum-general-stores which were on every street. Extremely good chocolate meant a single chocolate each from Dracula's.

'They're so wonderful,' said Wilf, hungrily. He could have eaten dozens if he'd had the money to buy them.

'Okay, we'll walk then, and go to Dracula's.'

It took about fifteen minutes to walk to Gastgate, even allowing for Wilf lingering longingly outside the dimly lit music shop. 'It's so old, you could imagine Brahms or Beethoven buying music here,' said Wilf.

I couldn't imagine either of these eminent composers ever setting foot in Doume, there must have been better places to visit, even then.

Gastgate was the main shopping street in Valderk. Main because the most sumptuous and unusual shops were there, not because it was a wide street full of trams and cars and buses. We slowed down when we got there: it's the sort of street where you can't walk fast as there's always something in the next window you want to see.

My special favourite is the skull shop. 'These people are nuts,' I said. There was a sensational window display of miniature china skulls with jewelled eyes, all displayed on swathes of purple velvet. Reasonable prices, too, but what could you do with them? Wake up and find one of those on your bedside table, leering at you, and you'd have a fit of the heebie-jeebies. Well, I would, anyway. One can only take so much, but they were lovely.

'Look over here,' said Wilf, dragging me over to the other side where a classy estate agent's window was full of photos of weird and wonderful castles and houses on sale for many hundreds of thousands of vlads. Interior shots showed staircases wide enough to drive a lorry up, or, alternatively, sinister stone spirals twisting up into the darkness.

'Those spooky towers are incredible,' I said, wondering who on earth lived in these castles.

The next shop along showed that the people of Doume loved their strange castles, even if they didn't have the vlads to buy a real one. It was a lamp emporium, and lots of the lamps featured castles. There was one with ghostly lights shining out through dozens of pointed windows, and another where a large bat-shaped lampshade was perched on a riot of spires and turrets.

'Cool,' said Wilf. 'Let's save up and buy one for Mum for Christmas.'

'I don't suppose they have Christmas here,' I said, as we wandered past a bookshop full of ancient, cobwebby tomes. 'Not like we do, anyway.'

'Hey,' said Wilf. 'Look at those.'

'They're different. Black and gold and dark red; it's unusual.'

'Blood red,' said Wilf. 'I wonder what they are?'

I thought for a moment, trying to remember what they reminded me of. 'I've got it,' I said. 'They're like those tea urns they have at functions. You see, each one has a little tap.'

'They don't look like tea urns to me,' said Wilf doubtfully.

'They're much more ornate, that's all. They would be, since they're Doumian.'

'Kind of samovars,' said Wilf after another good look. 'You could be right.'

There was a queue at Dracula's. There always was, and on a Saturday it seemed that half of Valderk wanted to buy chocolates. Wilf and I didn't mind. It was wonderful just standing there, sniffing the rich and delicious smell of chocolate which wafted out through the door. And it was fun to watch Doumians with more than their fares to spend buying chocolates.

Up at the counter, a woman with silver and purple hair was buying several boxes of bat mints. They were a lot different from After Eights or Bendicks best, since they were all thin mints in the shape of bats. Some had outstretched wings, some drooped in that way bats do. And some where just in the shape of a bat's head, with little crystals of mint for eyes and teeth.

I like mint chocolates, but I hadn't tried these, I wasn't too sure about biting into a lot of bats. But they were obviously popular with the locals. As were the chocolate teeth and the house speciality: chocolate eyeballs with marzipan topping. Customers were biting into these before they had even left the shop, going past us with satisfied crunchings.

We'd already made up our minds what we were going to have by the time we reached the counter. Wilf went for several links of orange chocolate chain, and I chose a dark chocolate heart. It came with a white chocolate flake embedded in it.

'I wonder what that's meant to be,' I said as we left the shop.

'A stake,' said Wilf, swallowing the last of his chain.

'Um,' I said, pulling it out and eating it first.

They were so good that we were tempted to buy some more. But that would have meant dipping into our pocket money, and we had other plans. Wilf wanted to buy a book, and I had my eye on a spectacular T-shirt I'd noticed in a shop window from a tram.

'We'd better get a move on,' I said as we left Gastgate and crossed Murke Square on our way to the less classy Grind Street. Wilf squinted up at the huge clock on the tower in the centre of the square. It wasn't easy to tell the time from it, because the hands were so curly and decorated, but we were getting the hang of Doumian clocks.

'We've got about half an hour,' said Wilf, finally, 'in order to give us time to get home by the time we said we would.'

'Always supposing the clock's right,' I said. 'According to my watch, it's twenty minutes out.'

'Ahead or behind your watch?' said Wilf.

'Behind.'

'Oh, rats,' said Wilf. 'We'd better get a move on.'

Fourteen

WILF THOUGHT I WAS MAD TO SPEND MY MONEY on the T-shirt, but I liked it a lot.

It was black, with eyes all over it, gold and green and silver and red. Wilf said it was creepy, but then Wilf isn't into fashion. Moreover, it was on special offer. I told him that I'd pay the fares on the tram with the money I'd saved; if we went home by tram he'd have time to choose a book.

You never know with Wilf. Sometimes he can spend hours brooding round a bookshop, as though there's nothing he wants to buy. Other days, he'll zip in, take a book from the shelf, and be straight out.

I hoped today was going to be a zippy day, because otherwise Mum would be cross. She was cross a lot at the moment; her mood hadn't improved at all. I'd never known her like this. She was missing Marks & Spencer and coffee with her friends, Wilf thought. This was simplistic, but I expect Dad thought the same. I knew what the real problem was, and why she was so fidgety. She was missing work, not M. & S. and friends. Mum hates having to depend on Dad for money. He can get very fussy about what she spends it on, so I don't blame her.

Today it seemed as though we were in for a zip, but just as Wilf was pulling out a fat paperback, he pushed it back. Oh, no, indecision time.

It wasn't. He came over to where I was standing by a carousel of Asterix books, sneaking a quick read. 'Look,' he hissed, jerking his head towards the Travel section.

'What?'

'Look who's there.'

A couple of students, sensible types, planning to leave Doume as fast as possible; a granny who looked like the passenger from hell; a soppy girl leafing through a copy of *Paris, City of Romance* . . . and a tall, thin, unremarkable man in round specs.

A familiar tall, thin man with specs. One whose face had been in the *Daily Doume*, peering out from behind Stuka.

'Rudi Drink . . .' I began, and then shut my mouth quickly as Wilf trod on my foot.

'You carry on with the Asterix,' he whispered. 'Look uninterested, but keep an eye on him. Maybe he's on the trail. Maybe he knows where the thief has gone, and is seeing how to get there.'

Not even the Doumian police could be that stupid, I reckoned, but it would be good practice to see what he was up to, seeing as how Foujay had enrolled us as Sergeant Plods.

Wilf went over to the travel books and started flicking through a book lying on the display table. I could see him watching Rudi D. out of the corner of his eye. The tall man put back the book he'd been looking at and moved away to another section. Wilf waited a minute or two, then left his book and followed him into the depths of the bookshop.

I stayed where I was.

Wilf fretted in silence on the way home, longing to pass on the results of his snooping, but unable to on the crowded tram. It was full; Doumians all seem to go about a lot on Saturdays, so we had to stand. He wouldn't say anything about what Rudi had been looking at until the tram screeched to a halt at our stop and we'd managed to get off.

'Near thing, that,' I said, getting my breath back. Citizens of Valderk are suspicious of you wanting to get off a tram before it gets to the end of the line. They crowd together rather than making a space for you to get out, and the driver's always in a hurry to be off again. It can be two or three stops further on than you want to be before you can escape, if you aren't careful. And forceful.

Wilf was deep in thought. 'Well?' I demanded.

'When he finished in the Travel section, he went over to Dictionaries,' said Wilf. 'Why dictionaries? You'd think a tourist language guide would be best, if he's planning a trip.'

I had been doing some thinking on the way home. 'Why was he lounging around in the bookshop anyhow? We know Dad's in the office, in the centre of the storm. So why isn't Rudi?'

'Make a note of it,' said Wilf. 'Foujay can work that one out; we've done our bit.'

I felt pleased with our morning's work. While Foujay had been visiting relatives, we'd kept on with the case, and gleaned some useful info about Rudi D. He didn't impress me, I have to say. If that's the way he works on a big case, the prisons in Doume must be empty. Perhaps he'd thrown in his hand, and was leaving it all to Stuka. It didn't matter. We had some concrete news to report to Foujay, and we'd done it without Dad's help.

Which wouldn't have been any help at all, as it turned out.

Apartments in Doume often have a concierge, a nosy party who lives on the ground floor and snoops on everyone's comings and goings. Ours was one Mrs Cavity. She was a stout number, with a mouthful of gleaming gold teeth and thick grey hair dragged back in a tight bun. She always wore boots, whatever the weather.

Wilf and I reckoned that Mrs Cavity had flourished under the last regime. Foujay said that she was a paid Secret Police informer, like all the other concierges in Valderk. Whether this was true or not, she seemed always to be on duty. She counted the residents and their visitors out, and she counted them in, and charged residents and non-residents alike two erks for having the door opened and for using the decrepit lift.

Mrs Cavity shot out of her den with a horrid smile pasted on her face and her hand held out for her erks. 'You'll be looking forward to going out with your pa tonight,' she said. 'They're showing *Fangs Two* at the Foxy, you'll enjoy that.'

I was very sniffy, saying that our father was likely to be busy. Wilf had made it to the foot of the staircase which spiralled round the central lift cage, and I slipped past Mrs C. to join him.

'No, he isn't busy any more,' she shouted triumpantly after us. 'He's been taken off the case.'

We whizzed back to her little cubbyhole, but before we could question her further she dived back into her lair and snapped the window shut with a hideous cackle.

Moody Rudi

What's up with the Police Chief Rudi Drinkwater? Is he sulking because yet again un-Secret Policeman Stuka has stolen the limelight?

At a state dinner last night to celebrate ninety-nine years of the Doumian police force, broody Rudi sat unsmiling, chain-smoking little black cigarettes and refusing to speak to any members of the press, including Gloria Smurk, *The Shout*'s representative at this glittering occasion.

Our distinguished Chief of Police is fed up, a little bird tells us, because he was missed out in last month's King's honours – yet again. Could be you're not solving enough crimes, Rudi. Get back our lost treasures, and *The Shout* will demand you get the recognition you deserve.

Meanwhile, here's *The Shout*'s advice to you, Gloomy Rudi – put a smile on your face, leave the white-tie scene to Stuka and co, and get out there after the villains.

Fifteen

FOUJAY TELEPHONED THAT EVENING, AFTER WE'D got back from the cinema.

We didn't go to the Foxy in the end. Instead, Dad took us into town to see an American film at the Metropole. I wondered what the Doumians made of it; it was all so *normal*. Car chases, drug addicts, a couple of serial killers, all ending in a blaze of gunfire.

Dad worried that he shouldn't have brought us. 'I didn't realise it was going to be so violent,' he kept on saying. 'There's no grading of films here, that's obvious.'

Wilf and I reassured him that we weren't about to go out and start a life of violent crime on the strength of having seen one film, but he went on muttering.

'Not many people here,' he said, as the thin audience trickled out. A woman in front turned round and flashed a pair of dark eyes at him. 'They're all at *Fangs Two*,' she said. 'That's a good film, you can really get involved. These American films are so strange, so improbable.'

'It's the Foxy for us next week,' said Dad firmly.

'*Grandson of Dracula* is coming on,' said the woman. 'That should be really good.' Then her companion dragged her off and she gave Dad a wink and went out into the street.

★

Foujay asked what we'd seen, and dismissed the American film as arty rubbish, which I thought was an original point of view. It was further proof of how differently Doumians see things.

He turned to the matter in hand. 'What did you get out of your dad? What's Stuka up to? And more importantly, what's Rudi doing?'

I looked round to check that Dad was firmly shut away in the sitting room before telling Foujay about Dad coming off the case. 'He's quite relieved, he says, because he's never seen such strange policework.'

Foujay groaned. 'Never mind about the finer points, how are we going to know where Rudi is and what line he's taking?'

Wilf and I had talked that over. 'You'll have to find out, from your auntie.'

'From Lulu?'

'Yes.'

Long silence.

I rattled the receiver, thinking we might have been cut off, which is something that happens all the time in Valderk. Either that or you find yourself having a conversation with a total stranger. That happened to me the other night, and the man invited me out to dinner and a show. Dad was quite shocked, and I was inclined to go along, just to see who it was, but the whole family vetoed that very quickly. Very unadventurous, my family.

'Don't do that,' said Foujay.

'Do what?'

'Make that crackling noise. It's deafening at this end.'

'I thought the connection was broken.'

'Well, it isn't. I was just thinking.'

'What's the problem?'

'You haven't met Lulu,' said Foujay glumly. 'She's got a mind of her own, and she'll only talk when she's in the mood. Which means when Stuka's annoyed her.'

'Does he do that often?'

'Every time he flirts with another woman. Which is a lot.'

More cracklings. I began to wonder if someone was listening in, and whether to mention this to Foujay.

He wasn't concerned. 'Probably. They do it all the time, out of habit. I don't think anyone ever listens to the tapes, though. As far as I know the playback machines all need spare parts.'

That was comforting.

Foujay's mind was still running on his aunt. 'I know, there's a concert on tomorrow. Lulu might be there. We could try and get the lowdown from her.'

Wilf had crept out into the hall, and was breathing down my neck, trying to hear what Foujay was saying. 'Concert?' he said, much interested.

'Jazz,' said Foujay.

Wilf lost interest, but I thought it sounded a good idea. Always supposing we could persuade Mum and Dad to let us go. Which wasn't very likely.

Luck was on our side. Mum and Dad were going out to dinner. Dinner with Mr Johnson. Our ears pricked up at that. 'I thought he was under arrest,' I said innocently. 'For taking the secret formula.'

'Pah,' said Dad, or something like it. 'They had to let him go.'

'All those connections?'

'Not a bit of it. Although he now works in the confectionery field, Mr Johnson is a lawyer by training. He wriggled his way out of it, as lawyers do. He's still

— 71 —

under suspicion, of course, especially as far as *The Daily Doume* and *The Shout* are concerned. He's had to surrender his passport and they've told him he must stay in Doume.'

'That's no problem,' murmured Wilf. 'I expect he could slip across the border with the smuggled salami if he wanted to.'

'What did you say?'

'Nothing, Dad. Just humming.'

Wilf and I had a plan. Mum and Dad were going to leave at about seven – they said. The concert, so Foujay had told us, began at half past seven. Luckily at the Café Nix, which wasn't far from our apartment. Wilf was torn. He doesn't like jazz, but he was longing to meet Lulu. Curiosity won.

Mrs Cavity always watches *Dark Nights*. It's the most popular soap here in Doume, and it's on three times a week. Then they do an omnibus on Sunday night. If she's missed during the week, she catches up on Sundays.

'It's a long shot,' I said to Wilf.

'Not so long,' said Wilf. 'It's on on Wednesdays, and that was the night when the people in the first-floor apartment had that terrible row. Bet she was at the door, listening.'

I hoped Wilf was right. We pushed Mum and Dad out of the flat by ten past seven. I'm surprised they didn't think something was up, we were so keen to get rid of them. In fact Dad was suspicious, but Wilf cleverly turned the telly on, and swore we were hooked on *Dark Nights*.

'I hope you've done all your homework,' said Mum. 'And no staying up late, it's school tomorrow. We'll be back by half past ten.'

'Plenty of time,' said Wilf, as we tiptoed down the last flight of stairs. We knew that the bottom step creaked; it had obviously been fixed that way by Mrs Cavity years ago, in order to let her know when residents were on the move.

We jumped.

And waited.

The door of the den stayed closed. From inside, we could hear high drama as *Dark Nights* went through its usual dose of betrayal and doom.

'Now!' said Wilf. 'Scuttle.'

Something in the air of Doume makes one good at scuttling. In seconds, we were past Mrs Cavity's door and outside in the dank air of a Valderk evening.

'This way,' said Wilf.

'Um,' I said. 'Wilf, do you remember the guidebook said Valderk wasn't safe after dark?'

Wilf looked up and down the dimly lit street. 'Let's hope they meant it wasn't safe for tourists,' he said, setting off at a good pace in the direction of the Nix.

'The guidebook said that the main danger, apart from the bats, is Lurkers.'

'Lurkers? Oh, for heaven's sake, that guidebook's total rubbish. Lurkers. I ask you.'

THE DARKSIDE GUIDE TO
THE KINGDOM OF DOUME

LURKERS

Otherwise known as **Hounds of Doume.** *Large, black, fanged dogs with thick black fur which lurk in the doorways of Valderk, hence their name. They jump out on unwary passers-by and attempt to draw blood from their limbs. This can lead to medical complications: if bitten, see a doctor. The only known Lurker deterrent is issued by Vurshka's Fangmacy and is partly composed of the common herb lurksbane, found in the deep forests during the new moon. You can recognise a Lurker from afar by the gleaming of its crimson eyes.*

Sixteen

AFTERWARDS, WHEN THE CASE WAS SOLVED, DAD said that you don't meet many Lulus in a lifetime.

One is enough.

Lulu is opulent. It's the only word for her. Voluptuous would do, Mum says, so I suppose she's that as well. Curvy. Very tall. Black hair, dark soulful eyes, a husky voice – you get the picture. My jaw dropped, I have to tell you, when I saw her sitting there at her little table, one very high-heeled and strappy sandal tapping with the beat.

'All her clothes come from Paris and Italy,' Foujay whispered in my ear as we sat perched on stools in a distant corner.

Since it was a concert, you needed tickets, but since Foujay was Foujay, one of the barmen was his sister's current boyfriend, so he sneaked us in for nothing.

I like jazz. I like the sound of the saxophones and the double bass and all that. The blues numbers make me feel sad, the lively ones make me tap my feet – what more could you want?

Wilf may not like jazz, but he knows about it. 'There's more to it than that,' he said disapprovingly.

I didn't want to know. I sat, and listened, and drank a strange concoction which Foujay's barman had rustled up for us.

'What's in it?'

Foujay opened his mouth, and then shut it. 'Best not to ask,' he said. 'Do you like it?'

'Mm, I do, quite.'

'Then that's all you need to know.'

Wilf was getting restless. 'When are you going to tackle this Lulu?' he asked Foujay. 'No point in our sitting here in this dark corner all evening. We're here to work, remember?'

'There'll be a break in a while,' said Foujay. 'Then we'll wander over.'

'What if Stuka turns up?' I asked. This Lulu was clearly not the kind of woman who was going to sit alone at her table all evening. There was another chair beside her, but it seemed to have a fur coat on it. Black. Grr. I totally disapprove of women who have furs. It confirmed my first, bad impression of Lulu.

'Stuka?' said the barman, who had long ears. He nodded at Foujay. 'Lulu's your aunt, isn't she?'

Foujay nodded.

'She came with Stuka. Then they had a flaming row. He said Keewee had bitten him, and Lulu told him not to be such a baby, and one thing led to another and Stuka left.'

Keewee? Did she have a dog? Under the table, probably, poor creature. I wouldn't be her dog for anything.

'Look,' said Wilf in awed tones.

I had misjudged Lulu. She didn't wear furs. The pile of fur beside her suddenly got up and stretched. A pair of huge golden eyes flashed open and shut again, and a large pink mouth opened in a yawn, displaying a splendid set of teeth including four fine fangs. Like any cat does, it extended its black legs and flexed its paws, its unsheathed claws much in evidence. Eek.

—— 76 ——

'That's Keewee,' said Foujay. 'One of the original fanged Doumian cats. They're very rare.'

'It's huge,' I said. It was, getting on for panther size. Only with silkier black fur – and, of course, the threatening dental fixtures. It wasn't the kind of animal which featured on TV pet programmes.

'Wow,' said Wilf, who liked cats. 'That is the biggest cat I ever saw. Those paws are enormous.'

'Yes, and claws to go with them,' said Foujay. 'He goes everywhere with Lulu, usually wrapped round her neck.'

The music stopped in a whirl of noisy chords. Wilf winced, and Foujay got up.

'This is our cue,' he said, slipping through the concert-goers like an eel, leaving me and Wilf to follow as best we could.

Lulu turned her head as Foujay came up. Her eyes narrowed, and she gave him a long, tough look.

'Did Stuka send you?'

'I haven't seen Stuka,' said Foujay. 'Is he coming to the concert?'

'He is not. He came, Keewee bit him, and so he went.'

'Went where?' said Foujay bravely, dropping into a chair from the next table. The people who were sitting there had made a rapid exit when they realised what Keewee was.

'To work,' said Lulu. 'Via the hospital.'

Wilf and I were hovering in the background. Foujay brushed his ear with his hand. A fly? I wondered.

'He wants us to listen and take notes,' said Wilf out of the side of his mouth.

I shrugged and turned my empty hands up, to show I had nothing to write on. Wilf drew out Foujay's note-book, which he'd collared when we left our corner.

Okay, so Wilf uses his brain. I, on the other hand, can

do shorthand. Which he certainly can't. Well, not proper shorthand, not the one that's all hooks and squiggles and loops. I tried that, but it defeated me utterly. So I went on to something called Quickwriting. I found a book on it in the library. It's neat, you leave out inessential letters.

Lk ths.

FJ: Wys KW lshng hr tl?

L: Shs hngry. Cl th wtr & sk fr plt chkn fr hr.

Reading it back, you get Foujay asking why Keewee is lashing her tail and Lulu telling him that she's hungry and to call a waiter and ask for a plate of chicken for her.

Easy, huh? It is when you know how, although I do get some strange sentences sometimes, if you aren't concentrating. I mean, Cl th wtr could be Cool the water, which would be quite different.

Context is all.

Foujay and Lulu talked, Wilf listened, and I scribbled. Goodness, what a gossip Lulu is. The things she said about people she knows, ears must be burning all over Valderk.

When we got home, I typed out my notes. I didn't do it on Dad's computer, partly because it hasn't worked properly since we arrived in Valderk, and partly because I didn't want traces left on the hard disk. So I used the little portable typewriter I've had since I was eight. It's best to write my shorthand out at once, because of strange sentences, like I said. We had to turn the lights out when we heard Mum and Dad coming in – half past ten indeed – but we went on with it when they'd gone to bed.

I left out the gossipy bits, but wrote it up so that it was interesting to read. I intend to work as a reporter when I grow up, and I thought that this was good practice. Wilf wanted me to include everything, but I think he's too young to dwell on that kind of scandal.

NOTES ON FOUJAY'S CONVERSATION WITH LULU AT THE CAFÉ NIX

Stuka is convinced that Johnson is the criminal. This is because
a) he is English
b) he is short of money
c) he is behaving suspiciously, leaving his house to make calls from boxes, looking round to see if he's being followed etc.

Lulu's comment: 'I'd behave suspiciously if I thought Stuka had his eye on me.'

Apparently, Stuka doesn't do things by half. He uses ten bugs when one would do, so you find microphones in the fridge and in your toothpaste. His idea of discreet surveillance is several men in black diving into doorways and slinking past you with sideways looks. As Lulu says, it's enough to make anyone jumpy, even if all they're doing is going out to buy a tin of cat food.

In fact, she said that one of Stuka's men accidentally put a tracer microphone on a tin of cat food – he mistook it for a tin of beans – and then the cat ate it. Stuka went wild with delight when the cat set off after dark across the roofs; he thought the suspect was meeting fellow-criminals in a noisy dive. Then the cat yukked it up, while sneaking through the back of the Foxy, and the listeners picked up all this dialogue off the screen. It was a crime thriller showing, so that really got them mixed up.

Wilf says this is irrelevant, but I think not; it shows that Stuka is not a man of reason and sense.

Rudi Drinkwater is supposed to be working under Stuka's direction, checking fingerprints, questioning witnesses (only there aren't any) and digging up any dirt he can find on Stuka's favourite suspects.

Stuka isn't pleased with Rudi, because he is away from the office a lot, and Stuka wants him where he can see him.

Stuka is convinced that most of the crimes are the work of an international syndicate involved in the theft of artworks to sell to museums in America for huge sums of money. He says that the disappearance of the Hand of Doume and the Zizzo theft aren't connected to the art robberies. He suspects an underground anarchist movement.

Lulu's comment: Nonsense. Anarchists? These days? You don't need to go underground to destroy the Doumian economy, the government's doing an excellent job on that already. And the stolen art treasures are all hot, how could any museums buy them? If the crimes

are unconnected, why are the same
fingerprints, not on the central
criminal records, found at all the scenes
of crime?

Rudi Drinkwater is sure that the crimes
are connected. Stuka thinks Rudi is
following up his own leads and keeping
his findings from him, Stuka.

This makes Stuka furious.

End of report.

Seventeen

W E HAD SNEAKED OUT OF SCHOOL AT LUNCH-
time, which is not allowed in Doumian schools,
and were eating our lunch in the nearby Zombie Park. It
was green and I thought it was quite pretty. Except for a
strange statue in the centre where the paths crossed,
which gave me the shudders.

'What's that?' asked Wilf, awed.

'Valderk Council put that up fifty years ago, in
honour of the Undead. That's why it's called Zombie
Park. There's a bench over there.'

Wilf and I didn't fancy munching away under the
gaze of those ghoulish figures, so we vetoed that one and
found another bench under a tree, out of sight of the
memorial.

Foujay skimmed through my account of what Lulu
said while Wilf catnapped and I yawned my head off.

'It wouldn't do for an official report,' he said. 'Far too
chatty.' He gave me a sharp look. 'Do stop yawning.
What's the matter with you?'

Foujay can be very annoying. 'I'm yawning because I
was up late, writing that out.'

'It shouldn't have taken very long.'

I was too sleepy to point out that deciphering my
shorthand is serious work. 'It's all there,' I said.

'No need to snap.'

Foujay was taking this detective business seriously, I

could see. If he wanted notes written up like a government circular, then he should have done it himself. Wilf said so, and told him that it was irrelevant how it was written as long as it had the info we needed.

Foujay hummed to himself, and gazed up into the green leaves of the tree we were sitting under. 'I think Rudi and Lulu are right,' he said at last. 'Those fingerprints must mean that one person was present at all the crimes, even if they don't seem to be the same type of crime. We can forget about Stuka's anarchists. Stuka must be the only policeman in the whole of Europe who still worries about anarchists. I bet he looks under his bed every night to see if there are one or two hiding there. No, Rudi's the one to watch. He'll be on the track of the right man, and if we want to be in on the action, then we'd best see what he's up to.'

'In on the action?'

'It's all experience,' said Foujay. 'And who knows, we may spot a clue they've all missed.'

It didn't seem very probable to me, and I wasn't sure I wanted to go haring round on Rudi's tail. Stuka might not be altogether wrong. It could be a gang – or syndicate, as he put it. I like a bit of excitement, but I have a clear sense of reality, and I know that thugs in real life are best left alone.

'Are you that much of a coward?' said Foujay nastily.

'Yes.'

Wilf flew to my defence. 'She is not a coward, just sensible. But don't worry, Beanbag, we're not going to find ourselves in a shoot-out.'

Famous last words.

'All we'll be doing is watching Rudi and exercising our logical faculties.'

Where does Wilf get these gems? 'I still say it's

impractical to trail round after Rudi all day,' I said. 'Anyhow, he'll be in his office.'

'Sharpen your wits,' said Foujay. 'Lulu says not. Lulu says he's out and about, on the trail. And we know he's not got his nose pressed to his desk, otherwise he wouldn't have been lounging round in bookshops, would he?'

Foujay had other news for us. He has a cousin, who is a monk in the Monastery of Vlad the Good. I was surprised to hear this; you imagine monks to be older than that, but Foujay said that he was a distant cousin, and that he was quite old.

'I'm going to go and see him tomorrow,' he said. 'To get a first-hand account of the break-in at the monastery.'

'We know what happened,' said Wilf. 'Someone stole the Craque of Doume.'

'He can fill in the details for us. Besides, Cousin Longfang wouldn't mention much to the police, especially not Stuka.'

Longfang? I couldn't believe my ears.

'Old family name,' said Foujay. 'He's descended from one of the original founder knights.'

'Why should he talk to you?'

'No problem' said Foujay. 'I'm family, and he's a dreadful gossip.'

'Anyway, you can't go tomorrow, there's school.'

'Oh, didn't you know?' Foujay sounded surprised. 'It's a holiday. We get two days off.'

'Why?'

'Feast of St Vlad the Good. That's always a two-day holiday.'

I liked the sound of this. 'Are there a lot of holidays in Doume?'

'Masses,' said Foujay. 'All the old Doumian ones, like

Vlad the Good, and the usual European ones, Christmas and Easter and May Day and so on. Then there are the ones that sprouted under the communists, and when the regime fell people didn't want to give up any holidays, so they just tacked on a few new ones to celebrate the new regime.'

Lots of holidays was a definite plus for the Doumian way of life. Two days off so soon after we'd started school was a real bonus. Well, one good thing, I thought; if Foujay was off to the monastery, then Wilf and I would have some free time to ourselves. It was not to be.

'You'd better come with me, Beanbag.'

'To take notes, I suppose.'

'Exactly.'

Huh. Why should I end up playing Dr Watson? I asked myself. Still, the monastery sounded interesting. I've never been to one that was still up and running. All the ones I've visited have been ruins.

A wary look came over Wilf's face. 'What about me?'

'You'll be on Rudi duty,' said Foujay.

'What, by myself?'

'No, with Hardhat.'

A Craque-ing Crime

WE WAS ROBBED, SAY MONKS

We broke into the Monastery of St Vlad's and carted off the Craque of Doume? Why is security at this great national institution so lax? Why is the building not open to the public, who want to enjoy the beauty of its architecture? Why do we have monks at all, and who pays the bills?

We have a right to know.

Was it the same gang who have lifted so many of our treasures? These precious objects belong to you, the people, only someone isn't looking after them on our behalf. We want action, and we want it now, Chief Stuka please note. And this cheeky crook left a dummy stone in place of the treasure – a large pebble with a message on it. What did it say? 'A present from Chesil Beach.'

Get praying, brothers – we want the Craque back where it belongs. Show us if you're worth your keep.

Otherwise, watch out. *The Shout* is watching you.

Eighteen

I MET FOUJAY OUTSIDE THE NIX, AS WE HAD ARranged.

As I said, it's near our apartment, so I walked. Dread Street, where we were, is a small street off what the Doumians call the Boulevard, and Wilf calls the Tunnel of Darkness. It's a wide road, with a central area between the lanes with shrubs and some sandy substance for you to walk on. There are benches for anyone who wants to sit and watch the cars and buses and lorries and trams rushing past. Valderk traffic is very smelly, and I shouldn't think you'd be very fit if you stayed there long breathing it all in.

On the outside of the traffic lanes are knobbly trees. Their leaves are a dark purple, and they are planted very close together. They are quite tall, and the upper branches hang over the road, hence Wilf and the tunnel.

I walked down the central area, wondering where I was going. Mum had asked me; she liked to know where I was. So I said sightseeing, and that seemed to satisfy her. But where was this monastery? It could be miles and miles out of Valderk, and I didn't think I had enough money for train fares. Even though Dad says travel in Doume is exceptionally cheap, it still costs money.

Even more than these practicalities, though, it was the whole enterprise which alarmed me. Keeping an eye on the great sleuth was one thing, but it looked as though Foujay was branching out on his own. Suppose by some lucky chance he did actually get near to the crook or crooks? Not a good idea; Doumian crooks in a hurry and laden with ill-gotten gains aren't likely to take kindly to a pack of intelligent young people on their trail. Oh, bother it; here I was, on a holiday, going off to this monastery to see some mad monk, it was too bad. Longfang indeed.

Foujay, hopping about with impatience outside the Nix, was more concerned about my clothes than about the monastery. 'Are you seriously going about in public wearing that T-shirt?'

I had my new many-eyed number on, and it looked terrific. Dad had winced when he saw it, and even Mum, who's fairly tolerant about things like that, blinked once or twice. But she didn't say anything.

'Good, isn't it?'

'Detectives are supposed to blend into the background.'

That is rubbish. Look at Sherlock Holmes with his caped tweeds and deerstalker and lung-threatening pipe, he was hardly one of the crowd. Then there's Poirot, with his moustaches and shiny shoes, and Morse with music blaring out of his old Jaguar. You'd instantly notice any of them if they came round the corner on a case.

I ignored Foujay's remark about the T-shirt and concentrated on the whereabouts of this monastery. Monasteries in Doume, it turns out, are always near towns.

Foujay obviously thought it would be pointless to be anywhere else. 'If they lived in the middle of nowhere, how would they get into town and make whoopee?'

'Monks aren't supposed to make whoopee.'

'Who says? Anyway, Doumian monks like to be near where the action is. It's only a tram ride on the number twenty-five from here, couldn't be easier.'

What a tram ride that was.

Most of the trams in Valderk travel from one side of the city to the other in a series of loops. Not the number 25. The 25 tram goes from our hilly part of the city, on the western side, straight down the Boulevard to the river, across the very shaky old tram bridge, through all the flat bits on the other side, past the football stadium and out towards the swamps.

'Whoever lives out here?' I asked Foujay, who was sitting with his eyes shut as the tram racketed along.

Everyone else on the tram had got out at the terminus on the edge of Valderk. The driver then changed the destination on the front to 'Outside Route', waited for a few minutes and clattered out again at the other end.

All I could see from the windows was a wasteland sprinkled with bright green grass which clearly indicated, don't mess about here. Sluggish streams, dank with drifting reed, ran alongside the tramway and across the flatlands. There were some strange bulrushes growing on the bank, with huge black heads, but even they seemed a bit subdued. There was no sign of any house or building of any kind.

The tram rattled into a deserted stop and ground to a noisy halt. Then it sat there, clicking away, while nobody got off or on.

I wondered if anybody ever used this stop.

'You never know,' said Foujay optimistically. 'Today might be a first.'

It wasn't and the tram finally clatter-banged on its way. The outlook began to improve, as the watery hell gave way to slight hills, and the tram crawled through cuttings, stopping at a wayside inn here and a straggling village there.

'However much further is it?' I asked Foujay, and at that moment the driver came to, rang a loud bell and called out, 'End of line, all change, St Vlad's Monastery.'

We got off, two monks wearing blood-red habits got on, and the tram rattled off back to Valderk.

'Monks usually wear black or brown where I come from,' I observed as we headed for an octagonal building set in the huge walls beside the vast wrought-iron gates. 'Or white,' I added.

'Very dull,' said Foujay. 'Here they're dark red or midnight blue. Now, don't say a word until we're inside.'

The gatehouse appeared to be deserted. It had a window in the side facing the gate, but this was covered by two heavily carved, pointy shutters.

'No one in,' I said hopefully. With every minute that passed, I felt more and more sure that we were on a wild-goose chase. Lucky Wilf, pottering about town with Hardhat. Rudi was probably browsing in bookshops again, which wouldn't exactly be a hardship for Wilf.

Foujay found a patch of shutter that wasn't carved with grinning, fanged creatures and gave several sharp raps. Then he stood back.

The shutters flew open and a gaunt figure appeared on the other side of a counter.

'And?' he growled.

'Come to visit Longfang,' said Foujay.

'Why?'

I would have apologised to the looming and terrifying monk and made a quick getaway, but Foujay was made of sterner stuff. 'He's my cousin. Family news.'

'Write to him,' said the monk, and slammed the shutters shut.

Nineteen

'WHAT A SOUR TYPE,' SAID FOUJAY. 'HARDLY good PR to have him on the door.'

He looked up and down the high wall which enclosed the monastery grounds. 'We could climb over.'

What a bad idea. Apart from the height of the wall, which was considerable, I could just imagine a line of gaunt-faced monks like the one behind the shutters waiting for us on the other side.

'They don't clone them, you know,' said Foujay. 'Most of them are quite normal and jolly. I expect they put him on the gate to frighten visitors away.'

'It works,' I said.

I was feeling very thirsty and fed up. All this way, and there probably wasn't another tram back into Valderk for ages. I asked Foujay about this.

'This afternoon is the next tram back to Valderk,' said Foujay helpfully.

I stood on one foot, trying to shake a stone out of my shoe. Then I lost my balance, and clutched at a bar on the big, ornate black gate to stop myself falling over.

The gate gave an evil squeak and swung open.

'Brilliant,' said Foujay. 'Quick, in we go, we don't want the gatekeeper to see us.'

I hesitated, not really wanting to be on the other side of the gate, but Foujay gave me a firm shove. 'Where's your spirit of adventure?' he said, setting off at a cracking pace along a travelled path. We hotfooted it until a bend, which took us out of view of the gate, and then Foujay slowed down to a normal pace.

'There's another of them,' I said, hanging back as I caught sight of a robed figure hard at work with a hoe in a large vegetable patch.

Don't imagine a cabbage patch, or neat rows of carrots and onions. Doumian vegetables, like so much else, are different. I have never seen red and yellow peppers that shape in my life; how can anyone eat them? And there were giant purple cauliflowers, and huge plum tomatoes. Dark red, to match the monks' habits, with very spiky leaves.

'They grow all this stuff for market,' said Foujay. 'You've probably eaten veggies grown here by the monks.'

I didn't like the thought of that.

'Can I help?' cried the monk, puffling slightly as we reached him, and he stopped hoeing.

He was short and round and should have been jolly, but he was looking very worried. As Foujay had promised, he seemed normal enough. Normal for Doume, that is.

'I've come to visit my cousin, Brother Longfang,' began Foujay.

The man clasped his chubby hands together and wrung them, emitting a kind of moaning sound.

Not normal, even for Doume.

'He's gone,' he finally said. 'Alas, alack, Brother Longfang has been snatched away, who knows where he may be? Perhaps the other world has sent a creature to take him from us, alack, alack.'

'What do you mean, gone? Has he gone into Valderk, or what?'

'No, no. Poor Brother Longfang has been confined to

his room with terrible gout. He can hardly hobble more than a step or two. And now he's gone. Snatched, leaving just a message, scrawled in the dust on his window-ledge.'

'Message?'

'I'll show you. If you are his cousin, you will have to break this dreadful news to your family.'

'Alack,' I added under my breath, as he set off at a brisk trot.

Foujay gave me a dark look, and followed the roly-poly monk. I trailed along after them at a gentle walking pace.

'Hurry up,' cried Foujay, turning round and flapping at me in a very irritating way.

I slowed down even more. I hate bossiness, and Foujay being the great detective was at his bossiest.

'Every second may count,' he said. 'Clues could be destroyed by the time we get there.'

Clues indeed.

I was at that moment passing under a tree. The branches were quite low, and as I ducked a huge black shape dropped out of the leaves, coming straight for me.

I gave an ear-splitting yell and ran, waving my arms to keep the black thing off. It was some kind of bird: a crow, a raven, a coal-black albatross . . .

The monk stopped at the screeching noises and looked round. 'Alack, alack. Brother Longfang's pet raven.'

Pet?

'I don't think he likes the eyes on your shirt. He's attacking them.'

Eek. Being dive-bombed by an outsized raven is a terrifying experience.

Once out of the branches, the dimwitted bird could see that these weren't real eyes. Nonetheless, he flapped and croaked along beside us; this time, I kept up with the monk and Foujay.

The monk took a sharp left turn and dived into a tunnel of murky shrubs. It had a damp and bitter smell. The tunnel ended in another arched door, set into a crumbling wall. The monk turned the great iron ring, there was a clang and a groan of hinges and it swung open.

The monk hurried through, followed by Foujay, me and the raven.

The three of them hurried on. I was so stunned by what was before me that I just stood stock-still and stared.

I mean, how could anybody, anywhere, any time, build something which looked like that?

Twenty

WHILE WE WERE ON MONASTERY DUTY, WILF WAS having a bewildering time with Hardhat.

He told me afterwards what had happened. It was clear that it was only luck things turned out the way they did. Luck, Hardhat's habit of bumping into things and Wilf's excellent hearing.

'Hardhat was really difficult,' Wilf said.

To begin with, Hardhat wanted to follow Rudi D. on his blades. Which, as Wilf told him was daft. If Rudi was walking, then Hardhat couldn't go slowly enough and would be bound to end up running his quarry over. And if Rudi hopped on to a tram, then what?

'I expect Hardhat would simply have hooked himself on to the back of the tram,' said Wilf. 'Besides, I wasn't going anywhere on blades, and Foujay had told us to stick together. So I vetoed the blades, and I wouldn't let him bring his skateboard, either. I told him to take his helmet off as well. Not very clever, trying to be inconspicuous with that thing on his head.'

'And he agreed?' I was surprised at that.

'No way,' said Wilf. 'So we lurked about a bit, and then Rudi D. came out and we set off after him. Keeping our distance, of course.'

Wilf was by this time beginning to feel very fed up, and thinking that the whole plan was a complete waste of time, just as I had. He said to Hardhat that Rudi would probably go to the market and then stop off at the cinema to watch the cartoons. Doumians of all ages love cartoons.

But Rudi didn't. He turned off at Murke Square, diving into the warren of old streets they have there. That's the mediaeval part of Valderk, full of fairy-tale half-timbered houses with the first floors on either side of the narrow streets jutting out over the street and practically touching each other. There are always people leaning at open windows and chatting to their neighbours on the other side. They hang lines between their windows, too, and you see some pretty strange sights in the underwear line when you walk about in that part of the city. Not to mention that the pegs aren't very well made, and when it's at all windy items of washing fall down and wrap themselves round your ears. Very different to street life in, say, Basingstoke.

Rudi D. obviously knows the city well, because he shot along, never stopping to peer up at the street names like everyone else has to. Hardhat pounded along beside Wilf, grumbling away about how he could keep up much better if Wilf'd let him bring his blades.

As I told him afterwards when he was still grumbling about it, with those cobbles he wouldn't have had any teeth left.

The south-west part of the city where they were is on the hilly side of town, with really steep streets, and Wilf found it hard work keeping up with Rudi D.

'I know where he's going,' said Hardhat suddenly. 'He must be going to Blud station. It's the first stop out of the terminus, on the way to the border at Csunya. My dad sometimes goes that way with a delivery.'

Delivery of what? Wilf thought it better not to enquire. Did it only go to the border, Wilf wanted to know.

No, there were lots of stations along the way, according to Hardhat.

Wilf sighed. If the train had been going straight to the border, he would have been able to call off the stalking then and there. They could hardly get on a cross-border train with no papers.

'He's not going to the station, he's going on up the street,' said Hardhat. 'No, wait a moment, he's turned left. There are steps which take you down to the platform.'

The street curved just there, with a low wall on one side, where it overlooked the railway line. Wilf peered over, trying to see if Hardhat was right, but before he could see who was on the platform, he heard the familiar banshee wail of a Doumian train.

He tugged at Hardhat's arm and hurtled down the steps. There was a ticket machine at the bottom, labelled 'Fangs and phillings only', no erks and perks. Wilf rummaged in his left-hand pocket where he kept his fangs, and fed in the coins for two half-returns to the border.

'Are we going to the border?' asked Hardhat, puzzled, as the train lurched into the station.

'I hope not, but this will cover us for all the stations. We don't know where he's going.'

They climbed up into the train, and spent a minute or so wrestling with the ticket-punching machine at the carriage entrance. It chewed up their tickets, only releasing any of the remnants when Hardhat gave it a hefty clunk with his fist.

'I hope the ticket collector doesn't come,' said Wilf, stuffing the shreds into his pocket. 'And I don't know what we'll do on the way back.'

'Nobody buys tickets on feast days,' said Hardhat, heaving at the sliding door which separated them from the next carriage. 'The ticket collectors don't work on holidays.'

'You might have told me before,' said Wilf in exasperation. 'I do wonder what goes on in Hardhat's head,' he said to me afterwards. 'I mean, he watched me spending good fangs on tickets, and never said a word.'

Hardhat took no notice of Wilf, but looked through the glass in the top half of the connecting door which still wouldn't open. He drew back with a dramatic gesture. 'He's in there,' he hissed. 'Our quarry.'

Wilf squeezed past Hardhat to have a look. There were only a handful of people: a family group, two women in black, knitting strange, pale woolly garments, a tough-looking man with vampire tattoos on his massive forearms, and a tall man in a white mac.

'Where?' said Wilf. 'Where is he? I can't see him.'

'Then you're blind,' said Hardhat. 'There he is, sitting by the window.'

Wilf looked again. The man sitting by the window wasn't Rudi D. It was the man in the white mac. And, now that he looked at him properly, he recognised him.

It was the Englishman from the airport. Stuka's chief suspect. Mr Johnson.

'That's not the one we're after,' said Wilf, roused to unusual temper.

'That's the one we've been following,' said Hardhat simply. 'And we aren't the only ones. Those two guys leering through the door at the other end of the compartment have been trailing him as well.'

'What?' said Wilf.

'Yes, all the way from police headquarters, where we picked up the man in the white mac.'

'We weren't following the man in the white mac,' said Wilf furiously. 'We're following Rudi D. Tall, specs and wearing a black coat.'

Hardhat thought for a moment. 'Oh, him' he said. 'Yes, he's been in front of us as well. This man, the one we're following, was following him. Even I could see that. And then those two men were following the white mac man as well. There's a lot of following going on all at one time. I wonder why everybody's doing it. It must be a craze.'

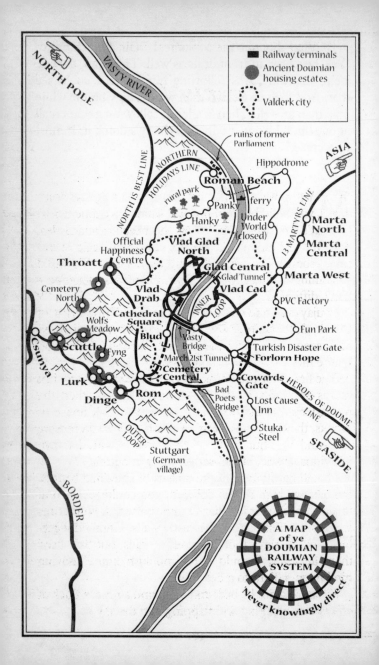

Twenty-One

M Y FAVOURITE KIND OF SANDCASTLE IS THE SORT you build by dribbling wet sand into exotic twirls.

That's fine when you're on the beach. Sandcastles, however grotesque and ornate, are small-scale structures, soon to be washed away by the tide. To build something like that full size, out of dark purple stone – that's different.

Foujay and the fat monk surged on, little cries of 'Alack, alack' wafting into the air. I just stood and gazed and gazed at the extraordinary construction which stood before me.

The first thing that knocked you sideways was its size; it was enormous, towering over you. Even when the monastery was thriving, and there was a full house of monks, they must have rattled around. Then there were the windows, hundreds of them, each with its own individual shape, but all rather wavy in outline.

I could hardly take in the dozens of spiralling turrets, the narrow, high doors, covered, you could see even at this distance, with familiar Doume carvings. Numerous staircases wound about the castle walls. Highly dangerous, I would have thought, with no rails, but they used them all right; I could see a monkish figure moving nimbly up a flight to a bell tower.

As he reached the bell, and unwound a rope, a flock of crows rose croaking and flapping into the sky.

Dong.

Foujay was nearly at the monastery building when he turned round and saw me rooted to the spot.

'No time for sightseeing,' he yelled. 'Get a move on, this is serious.'

Dong.

I headed for the door into which Foujay and monk had just disappeared. Up three wide steps, and through the open door.

It slammed shut behind me. We were in some kind of lobby, in a lofty, narrow space which soared up into one of the towers. The bell donged on, louder than ever as it echoed about the stone walls.

'This way,' said Alack, and headed for one of ten or so identifical passages which led off the lobby. I moved quickly after him and Foujay. I felt I would lose my reason if I got lost in this place. The monk hurried along flagged passages, up twisted staircases, along eerie galleries, through doors, round corners.

We'll be back at Valderk at this rate, I thought, when he stopped beside an open door and gestured dramatically at us.

'You see? His cell. Empty, alack, alack. No sign of Brother Longfang. Where can he have gone? Have the Dark Ones come out of the forest and carried him off?'

'I doubt it,' said Foujay, clearly startled. 'I don't think the Dark Ones would want to have anything to do with my cousin.'

I didn't ask who – or what – the Dark Ones were. I didn't at all like the sound of them, and a glance at the forest which I could see looming at the edge of the monastery grounds, a grim, black line of impenetrable trees, made me shudder.

'Here's the message he left,' said the monk, pointing to the window-ledge.

Foujay and I went over to the window. Brother Longfang did all right as far as comfort went. His room was a good size, and the windows were wide and well-made, once you got used to the odd shape. To my surprise, after all those stairs, we were on the ground floor. I wouldn't have cared for the view of the forest, but perhaps Longfang had a mind above the fears and frights of the rest of us.

Foujay was looking down at the word scrawled in the dust on the window-ledge. I couldn't make it out, and I was leaning forward to get a better look. Foujay put out a hand to hold me away.

'It says "Help",' he said. 'And look, a perfect set of fingerprints.'

That was careless of the kidnapper. Or perhaps they were Brother Longfang's. Or one of the other monks had made them when leaning out of the window, no doubt to see if Brother Longfang was lurking beneath the window-ledge.

'No, they aren't Longfang's,' said the monk. 'It's a right hand, you see, and Brother Longfang was missing two fingers on that hand. A vicious bat had a go at him, years ago now. Fortunately, he was left-handed.'

'Fingerprints,' said Foujay. 'It seems to me that there are an awful lot of fingerprints in this case. Too many perfect sets, and all the same. Have you called the police?'

'Yes. Chief Inspector Drinkwater came first thing this morning, and his officers are on their way now.'

'When did you notice my cousin was gone?'

'This morning, but we think he was taken yesterday. His evening meal was left outside his cell last night, as is our custom for sick brothers. It was there this morning. Untouched. Except for the odd bits which had been nibbled by creatures in the night, of course.'

Of course.

I find all these dark asides in Doume very frightening. It's a place full of the unknown and unexpected, that's what gets me. If you're in a country where there are tarantulas, for example, then you know what they look like, and you keep clear of them.

If all you know is that outside the door there might be a nameless black creature with glowing eyes, that's much worse.

Monk Alack was still yakking. 'All our community are out searching for your cousin. Except for Brother Crossbow, who is in the library, muttering good riddance, and laughing. He didn't get on with your cousin. And Brother Claymore, who rings the bell, as we always do when a monk is ailing or in trouble. He can't be released from that duty, it's a penance. And I stayed behind to let the police in and to inform the family.'

He gave a mirthless smile of relief. 'Only I've done that now, since I've told you. You're family. You'll do.'

'Yes,' said Foujay.

I could see he was thinking hard.

He looked around the cell. 'Are all his books here?' he asked suddenly.

'Alack, I cannot say. Although he does usually have a huge book in Old Doumian in here, and I don't see it. I should think Crossbow will have heaved it back to the library. Not that he can read it. Only Brother Longfang can read Old Doumian properly. He was teaching a lad from the village, but it takes a long time to learn.'

While the wailing brother was wringing his hands – I was beginning to suspect he was really enjoying all the excitement – Foujay's keen eyes had spotted something on the floor under the window. 'Goodness,' he said, pointing out of the window. 'Isn't that a black-fronted Gloome Heron? Very rare, aren't they?'

The monk looked intently out of the window, and while his attention was distracted, Foujay quickly bent down and picked up the object which had caught his eye.

The monk turned round to us again, shaking his head in disappointment. 'If it was the heron, I must have missed it, alack. Of course, you have young eyes, I expect you're right. It's a pity, I should like to have seen a Gloome, they are indeed rare, very rare.'

Foujay was lost in thought. I was longing to know what he'd picked up, but his face gave nothing away. He came out of his reverie. 'Back to Valderk,' he said. 'No time to lose. We must find out if those are the same fingerprints as in the other cases. Rudi must have photographed them when he came this morning.'

'How?'

'Your dad must know someone in that department. Or Lulu can find out for us.'

'Surely the case will be handed over to the local police force. Why should it have anything to do with the other cases?'

'Too much of a coincidence, another perfect set of prints. I'll bet anything they'll be the same as in the other crimes. No, no, Stuka will take one look and decide it's for him, let loose his Secret Police hounds on the monastery, I daresay they'll be here any minute. Monks? Internal security he'll say. He always has a finger in the pie when it's a bizarre high-profile case.'

I wondered if any cases in Doume weren't bizarre.

Foujay was peering up and down the corridor. 'Is that another cell next door?'

'No, that's a storeroom.'

'Has it got a window?'

'Yes.'

'We'll go that way.' He opened the door, pushed me

in, shut the door behind him and edged past a line of witchy brooms to the window. 'Quicker this way,' he said. 'Out you go.'

'No,' I said, standing my ground. 'Not until you tell me what you found.'

Foujay delved in his pocket, and handed me a little enamel brooch. It was in the shape of a bumblebee, and I recognised it at once. A big confectionery company in England had run a campaign for a new honey-flavoured chocolate bar last year, the Bee Bar. If you collected so many wrappers, you could send off for a pin or a brooch.

'I didn't know you had these in Doume.'

'I've never seen one like it before,' Foujay said. 'Have you?'

'Oh, yes,' I said, and was about to fill him in when a knocking sounded at the door, and we heard Alack's worried tones enquiring if we were within.

'Out,' said Foujay. 'Tell me later.'

Twenty-Two

A S WE RAN ACROSS THE LAWN TO THE GATES,
Foujay started to beep.

'That's a loud watch,' I said, as he skidded to a halt.
He gave me a supercilious look (Foujay is very good at
curling his lip) and pulled a mobile telephone out of his
pocket.

'Where did you get that from?'

'It's my mum's. Hardhat borrowed his dad's, so we
could keep in touch. In an emergency.'

He slid the aerial up and clicked the phone on. 'Hello.'

He listened to the voice quacking on the other end, his
face more and more puzzled-looking. Then he cut into
the stream of words. 'Get off the line, Hardhat, I can't
understand what you're going on about. Put Wilf on.'

He listened, then shook his head. He held the phone
away from his ear and shook it. Then he listened again.
'Where exactly are you? Why do you suppose anybody
would . . .? All right, all right. We're on our way back to
Valderk now. Over and out.'

He snapped the aerial down and tapped the phone.
'Very useful in principle,' he said, 'but not so good when
people talk rubbish.'

'Wilf doesn't talk rubbish.'

We had kept on walking while Foujay was on the
phone, and we were on our way out of the gates when we
heard the clang-clang and distant rattle of a tram. Foujay

broke into a run. 'We've got to catch it,' he shouted over his shoulder. 'Move.'

We reached the tram stop just in time. The tram drew in, and disgorged two monks in their familiar red habits, and a swarm of secret policemen. You could tell that's what they were because they had bands on their arms saying SECRET POLICE.

One of them, some novice eager beaver, immediately tried to arrest us, but Foujay was too quick for him, and he leapt on board the tram. I ducked and jumped on after him, the doors banged shut, the driver gave a defiant toot and we were off.

'What was all that about?'

'Stuka's mob. They arrest everyone they see any-where near the scene of a crime. All those monks will be behind bars tonight.'

'They won't cough up fines for Stuka.'

'You'd be surprised, they've got stacks of money, these monks, and they won't fancy prison food. They'll pay.'

'Good thing the driver got going.'

'Tram-drivers are suspicious of policemen in general and SKULK officers in particular. Tram-drivers are always getting parking tickets from the Secret Police mob.'

I was wondering how you gave a tram a parking ticket, and *why*, and looking peacefully out of the window when Foujay dug me in the ribs and commanded me to explain about the bee.

'The bee? Oh, the *bee*. The brooch.' I told him about the Bee Bar.

'Very interesting,' said Foujay. 'They don't sell these Bee Bars in Doume. I wonder how this bee got into Longfang's cell?'

'A visitor must have dropped it.'

'What company does Mr Johnson work for?'

I stared at Foujay. 'I don't know. Oh, wait a minute, Dad said something about his work. I know, confectionery and soft drinks.'

'Aha.'

'Aha, what?'

'I bet he works for the company that makes these Bee Bars. They sound disgusting, by the way. Far too sweet for my taste. But if it's Mr Johnson's company that makes these bees, then he might very well have some with him. People in companies often carry their promotional items about with them.'

'Do they?' I was sceptical about the connection. Even if it was his company, would he really be likely to have a brooch in his pocket? He'd hardly wear it, would he? And if he did have one on him, why should he drop it, and there of all places?

Foujay took no notice of my doubts, telling me that it was all a matter of probabilities, and the first rule of detection was to distrust coincidences. Then he instructed me to get out my notebook. 'You must write down what happened here. What the monk said, and the message and the fingerprints. Everything.'

I kept the cap firmly on my pen.

'Not until you tell me what Hardhat and Wilf have been up to.'

Foujay frowned. 'I wish I knew. There was Hardhat burbling on about a man in a white mac being on the tail of Rudi Drinkwater. Wilf wasn't any better. He said the same thing, and that the man was Mr Johnson. I told him he was in a muddle, Rudi must be trailing Mr Johnson, not the other way round. But he wouldn't have it.'

'If that's what Wilf says is happening, then that's

what's happening. Wilf may be a daydreamer, but he wouldn't be wrong about that.'

'It doesn't make any sense,' said Foujay, swinging his legs up on to the seat. He sank his head on to his knees, and did some tuneless whistling through his teeth.

'Stuka's men were there, too,' he said finally.

I was doubtful about that. Wilf and Hardhat would recognise Rudi D. and Mr Johnson, but how would they know who were Stuka's men?

'No problem,' said Foujay. 'Hardhat can spot one of those plain-clothes guys a mile off. He knows a lot of them, anyhow, because of them arresting his dad and uncle so often.'

'All in the family,' I said.

'We've got to think this one through,' went on Foujay. 'Question One, what is Rudi D. up to? My guess is that he's trying to find out where Cousin Longfang's been taken.'

'The police were only just arriving when we left. Wouldn't he wait until they'd taken statements and so on?'

'Those are the backup team and the security heavies. Rudi D. was there first thing, that monk said so.' He gave me a stern look. 'You aren't writing anything down.'

I gave in, and took the cap off my pen.

'Question Two: why is Mr Johnson following Rudi D.?'

I wrote that down, and chewed the end of my pen. A bad habit, since I often end up with black patches on my lips and tongue. Still, I don't suppose anyone would notice in Doume, they'd just take it for a new shade of lipstick.

In my opinion, Foujay was barking up the wrong tree. He'd misheard what Hardhat and Wilf were saying. You know how those mobile phones are, crackle hiss, and a voice coming at you from the end of a long tunnel. Clearly, Rudi D. was following Johnson.

Foujay would have none of that. 'No,' he said. 'Rudi's got a deep scheme. He's a great detective. He does the unexpected, and does it in unexpected ways. All the great sleuths are like that.'

I told Foujay he was out of date, that he'd been watching too many old films and detective reruns on the telly. 'Cops these days are all tough and hard and violent. They don't think, they just slam in there and get their man.'

'Crude,' said Foujay scornfully. 'And very unrealistic. It's brainwork that counts, every time.'

Oh, yes? In which case, why were we pounding about the countryside, instead of sitting and doing some serious and logical thinking.

'You've got to do the groundwork first,' said Foujay airily. 'Then we assemble all our notes and sift through the evidence. Then you see the pattern, work out who is the only suspect who could have committed the crime, unravel how he or she did it, and you're home and dry.'

Home and dry sounded good. The skies had been getting darker and darker, and now streaks of rain were running down the tram windows. I moved away from the window. Trams in Doume aren't exactly watertight.

The tram stopped, and a damp couple got on. The driver announced the stop, telling all four of us that this was Dinge, and to change here for the Loop, even while he was pinging his bell and revving up for a quick getaway.

Foujay sprang to his feet and told me in a ferocious voice to get up at once. 'Stop!' he yelled at the driver, who was so astonished that he did. Foujay tugged at the handle which slid the tram doors open, and two seconds later we were standing by the line as the tram swayed across the points and into the distance.

'Brilliant,' I said crossly. I had stabbed myself with my pen in the rush, and I didn't appreciate being startled like that. 'What was that in aid of? Were those two who got on spies in disguise? Hit men on the lookout for us, I suppose.'

'No,' said Foujay. 'It was the driver mentioning the Loop. That's what we need to take. Then we can join up with the others and really be in on events.'

So much for brainwork.

The Daily Doume

64 monks arrested in police swoop

The elite troops of SKULK yesterday arrested all the monks at St Vlad's Monastery. They are investigating the mysterious disappearance of Brother Longfang. Chief Stuka claims that Brother Longfang has been kidnapped. The police statement says that the criminals are either art thieves, the formula thief or aliens. Police are examining fingerprints discovered at the scene of crime.

The police haul included the great bell of the monastery, which came attached to Brother Claymore, and a large wild bird, which was also arrested and is being detained at Valderk zoo.

A tram driver and three passengers are also being held at police headquarters.

Twenty-Three

L ET ME EXPLAIN ABOUT THE LOOP.
Like most capital cities, Valderk has several main
railway stations, each one serving a different area of the
country. It isn't as simple as it might be, because the
termini are all in the centre and very close to each other,
and so you can't easily tell which one goes where. The
main station of Vlad the Cad, for example, is on the east
side of the river, but you take trains there to go to the
north-west of Doume, whereas Vlad the Glad Central is
to the north and you go from there first south and then
cut across the corner of the city to head out in a north-
easterly direction.

All the main stations are connected by the circular
Inner Loop train, known as the Circular. Outside the city
there is another circular line, which runs a complete ring
round Valderk, connecting with all the other main lines
several stops out from the city. This is the Outer Circular
which is known, since this is Doume, as the Loop.

The Loop connects with the main line from the
central station of Vlad the Drab (trains for the south-
west and the nearest border) at the station called Dinge.
This is a popular line, as it provides the quickest way out
of Doume.

I hope this is all now quite clear. I consulted a railway
map after the whole affair was over, just to check the
details, so I know it's right.

To get to the Loop platform at Dinge, which is both a tram stop and a railway station, you have to:

cross the tramlines;

walk alongside the railway track to the railway bridge;

walk across the railway bridge over the River Dribble, hoping that no trains are coming, since you have to walk on the actual track;

go through a damp and evil-smelling tunnel;

and finally emerge exhausted at the far end of a very long platform.

Foujay thought this was a very good connection, which made me wonder what the other connections were like. We hadn't been in Doume long enough to have done much rail travel, although Dad was always threatening us with it. I thought I'd tell him about Dinge, that'd put him off.

The station was deserted, with an iron bar – easily removable – holding the hatch down on the ticket office.

'Do we pay on the train?' I asked Foujay. This was a worrying thought, as I didn't have much money.

'I've got a book of tickets,' said Foujay. 'We just punch two of them when we get on. Although we won't need them, not on a public holiday.'

I went to look at the ancient and, as it turned out, unreadable timetable. It was pinned to an iron post with decorative bunches of grapes wound round it.

The station designer had obviously been keen on grapes, because more bunches of iron grapes hung from the platform canopy and what must have been meant to be a vine ran up the sides of the rickety bench outside the closed waiting-room.

Foujay wasn't bothered about the timetable. 'All lies, even if you could read it,' he said. Apparently the trains went round and round the circuit, and came every ten or fifteen minutes.

Foujay was planning ahead. 'Wilf and Hardhat were at Scuttle when they rang. That's two stations down the line from here. They'd just got off the train, and so had all the others.'

I couldn't see how we were going to meet up with them. 'Is Scuttle a big place?'

'No. It isn't anything much, a small village in the shadow of Castle Scuttle, which is a ruin. I think there are some workshops and industrial units there now.'

It didn't sound very promising, and I told Foujay so.

Foujay wasn't bothered. Foujay never did seem to be bothered. It must be pleasant to know you're always right.

'Rudi D. must have some lead, perhaps he's going to interrogate someone in the village. Or maybe chief suspect Mr Johnson has connections there.'

'Why should he?'

'There has to be some reason why Johnson is heading there. And, ah, I've got it, Rudi D. wouldn't have to follow him, because he knew all along where he was going.'

'How?'

'He's a detective. It's his job to know where suspects are going.'

I thought about this. 'You mean nobody was following anyone, they were just going to the same place?'

'Could be.'

'And Stuka's men?'

'Stuka's men will follow anything that moves.'

So much for mistrusting coincidences. I nearly said this to Foujay, but I knew he'd wriggle out of it somehow.

We'd had the platform to ourselves, but now some other people were coming along. They'd probably been lurking somewhere out of the rain, because the moment they'd arrived there was a series of clanging noises from a nearby signal box.

They all stood on the very edge of the platform, toes over the edge, peering along the line. The train arrived in a rush, and they all jumped backwards, swearing Doumian curses, and one or two or them shaking a fist at the grinning driver.

A guard jumped down on the platform. The platforms in Doume are very low, and the trains are a good way up from the ground. There was a great deal of pushing and heaving to get everybody aboard. A plump, baldheaded man in a brown hat was sent flying by the guard into a compartment with a well-aimed shove at his rotund rear. You could hear his indignant protests all along the platform, but it encouraged the others to move fairly smartly.

Foujay hauled himself on board, and then put down a hand to help me up. A thin, cross-looking woman nipped in front of me, and passed him a basketful of grumbling, cackling hens, followed by a couple of large hams.

The train was making impatient leaving noises, and the guard had hopped back on and was waving a green-spotted flag at the driver.

'Hey, wait for me,' I shouted, as the train began to move. I got a hold, Foujay heaved, and I landed in an undignified heap on the floor inside. Foujay hastily slammed the door shut as the train swayed round a curve and all kinds of things began to slide towards it.

We seemed to have clambered into a luggage van, since as well as fending off the hens, I found myself face to face with a surprised-looking goat. Sitting on a large box further along was a man with a strange black dog. It seemed to have dreadlocks, right down to the ground, and was almost completely square. You couldn't tell where the creature's head was until one end snapped at us as we edged past.

'That's a Doumehound,' said Foujay. 'They're related to the Hungarian Puli, and they're very intelligent.'

I doubted it.

The next compartment didn't have any wildlife in it, which was a relief, but it was very basic and not exactly comfortable. There were two long, bench-like seats running down each side, three central poles for standing passengers to cling to, and that was it. The seats were all taken, so Foujay and I clung.

'Couldn't we try another compartment?' I said to Foujay.

'No point,' he said. 'People will get off at the next stop, and we can get a seat then.'

'Are all the compartments like this?'

'Oh, no,' said Foujay. 'We're in first class here.'

So I shut up and concentrated on keeping my balance. I found that if I craned my neck, I could just see out of the window over the heads of the passengers on the bench. I hadn't seen much of the countryside around Valderk, except for the marshy wasteland we'd gone through on the tram, and I was surprised to discover that it was green and quite pretty.

'Vineyards,' said Foujay, jerking his head to the other side of the train. There were hills there, terraced from top to bottom and planted thickly with warped, tough-looking little trees.

'This is where the best Doumian wine comes from,' he told me. 'It's called Bat's Blood.'

It was an unwise remark, because now the other passengers came out of their travellers' trance and started to argue about wines. They all had their favourite type from their favourite region, and they all supported them at the tops of their voices.

'What a din,' said a disgruntled-looking man in the corner. He folded his lips and glared at the others. 'I'm a beer-drinker myself,' he announced.

I was thankful when the train began to slow down.

'We're coming into Lurk,' said Foujay.

Half the compartment got to its feet, still arguing about wines and abusing the beer-drinker. They pulled bags down from the bulging overhead nets, dumped cases and parcels on my and Foujay's feet, and then all fell in a heap as the train-driver accelerated into the final stretch before the station and applied the brakes with a terrible screech.

Twenty-Four

THE HEAP OF PEOPLE SORTED ITSELF OUT. ONE BY one, complaining and rubbing bits of themselves that they'd landed on, they climbed down on to the platform.

I could see the goat being passed down, much to its dissatisfaction if the vigorous kickings were anything to go by. The woman and her hens got off, too, and the dog lolloped off down the platform with its owner.

'Phew,' said Foujay. 'Not many people getting on here, thank goodness. Grab a seat.'

Only one person got into our compartment, and she came through from the next one; she hadn't joined at Lurk. I stared as she came neatly through the door; how did she manage it on those high heels?

'Auntie Lulu,' said Foujay, as surprised as I was.

We needn't have worried about seats. Keewee was travelling too, and as he sprang into the compartment all the remaining passengers rose and vanished along the train.

'Never fails,' said Lulu, arranging herself on the bench opposite us, and patting the seat beside her. 'I saw you getting on at Dinge, so I thought I'd come and find you.' Keewee jumped up, swung his big black tail round himself, yawned, showing those terrifying fangs, and blinked his great eyes at us.

'Bunch of idiots,' said Foujay, getting up and stroking

Keewee's velvety head. 'You're just a big, harmless pussy cat, aren't you?'

Rumbling purrs echoed round the compartment.

Some pussy cat. I think sabre-toothed cats should be in the wild or in a zoo. Not sitting just across the way from me.

Foujay was interrogating his aunt. 'Why are you travelling by train?' he asked her.

It was a good question, because Lulu didn't seem to be a train person.

'Road blocks,' she said, getting out a mirror and checking her perfect face. 'Stuka's put up road blocks everywhere. Mr Johnson has given his men the slip.'

I opened my mouth to tell her that they were still on his tail as far as we knew, when Foujay gave me a savage look and a none-too-gentle kick.

'Are you going to Valderk?'

I didn't know the Doumian railways very well, but I did know that the Loop was hardly the quickest way into Valderk. Round it, yes. To it, no.

'I'm going to Scuttle,' said Lulu.

'Oh, really,' said Foujay. 'So are we. We're meeting friends.'

'I'm meeting Stuka, and changing for the train to the border. We're going to stay with friends on the other side.'

'Stuka's in Scuttle?'

'He'd better be,' said Lulu. 'I don't like people who are unpunctual.'

Lulu may look fragile, but I was starting to think that Lulu was one tough cookie.

Foujay made a little humming noise. I knew exactly what Foujay was thinking. He was thinking that if Hardhat clapped eyes on Stuka, he'd probably take off into a nearby forest or dive on to any handy train. Wilf wouldn't be able to stop him.

The train had been rattling along in quite a normal manner, but all of a sudden it began a series of slowings-down and speedings-up and jerks and swayings which made me wonder whether it had developed square wheels.

'We're coming into Scuttle,' said Lulu. The train shot through the station, gave a wild whistle, came to an abrupt halt and then, very slowly, backed into the station.

Foujay looked out of the window. The platform was empty; well, he could hardly expect Hardhat and Wilf to be standing there waiting for us. After all, as far as they knew, we were back in Valderk.

Stuka wasn't there either. A little frown crept across Lulu's smooth brow as Foujay helped her down.

Scuttle was not the kind of station which made you want to linger. We looked up and down the platform. A sign saying WAY OUT pointed directly towards the ground. Another, MAIN LINE THIS WAY, had little hands at both ends, each pointing in a different direction.

'I'll go over the footbridge and wait for the border train,' said Lulu.

You could tell that she wasn't a happy bunny. Stuka might be a big cheese, but I felt he was going to regret not being on time.

'Have a good holiday over the border,' said Foujay, waving to her as she tripped along the footbridge.

She leant over the railing. 'If you see Stuka, tell him I'm catching the train to the border whether he's here or not. And if he doesn't make it, then I'll be calling my friend Rodney when I get there.'

Foujay gave her another wave, and hustled me out of the station. He looked quite pale.

'Is she mad?' he said. 'Does she seriously think I'd give Stuka a message like that? He'd arrest me on the spot.'

'Who's Rodney?' I wanted to know.

'One of Lulu's ex-boyfriends. Stuka gets jealous very, very easily.

'Lulu should watch it.'

'Lulu doesn't give a damn,' said Foujay approvingly.

Twenty-Five

A TRACK WITH DEEP, DRIED-MUD RUTS RAN PAST the station entrance. To our right, it disappeared up towards the wooded hills that were all around us. The other way led towards a grim black fortress, with gaunt, ruined ramparts silhouetted against the sky.

'This way,' said Foujay, setting off, needless to say, in the direction of the castle.

I rather liked the look of the road to the right. It would have seemed preferable to the other direction even if it had been labelled 'This way to the salt mines.'

'Hurry up,' said Foujay. 'They're all here somewhere, my instinct tells me so.'

'All?'

'Rudi D., Mr Johnson, Stuka, Stuka's men, and, of course, Wilf and Hardhat.'

'Why not Cousin Longfang while you're about it?'

'Could be, could be. Mr Johnson might have kidnapped him. In fact, if he's the Master Criminal, then he certainly did. Come on, the game is afoot.'

'Okay, Sherlock,' I said, trying to sound cheerful, although in fact I was scared. I didn't like this place at all. Too remote, too far away from civilization. And where was Wilf?

Foujay set off at a cracking pace. It wasn't raining here, and judging by the dust our feet were stirring up as we walked along the track, it hadn't rained recently at all.

'Which is a pity,' said Foujay.

How could it not raining be a pity? You can tell Foujay's never lived in England.

'We might have been able to follow footprints. Hardhat's got pretty big feet, and those funny trainers he wears have very unusual soles. We could spot them at a glance.'

Not such a daft idea, then. I looked hopefully down at the ground, but anything or anyone could have walked or driven along there without leaving any trace.

'How did the castle get ruined?' I asked Foujay. Mind you, it seemed like the best thing for it. Whoever would want to live in a place like that?

'The original castle was built by one of the first knights,' said Foujay. 'Baldric the Ill-Omened. He was a gloomy fellow, and they say he regretted not getting to the Crusades and killing everybody. Still, he had quite a good time here.'

'Good time? No, don't tell me.'

'His descendants were all more or less as nasty and gloomy as he was, and come the revolution, the local forces had a go at the castle. They were given a hand by some foreign troops that had wandered across the border to help with the revolution. They wanted to raze it to the ground, but that would have been a life's work.'

'I see. What happened to the Baldric family?'

'Oh, they hopped it across the border where the foreign troops had come from. Very harsh regime they had going then on the other side of the border. Just the Baldrics' cup of tea. Plenty of oppression. I think they'd have liked to come back, though, when that regime fell, but the new government weren't exactly keen on having them back.'

'So the castle's uninhabited?'

'Not exactly. That's where the workshops and factory units are, the ones I told you about. Oh, and a whole crowd of rather grisly ghosts.'

Ghosts?

I already felt that I was trying to make my way in unknown and dangerous territory, without a map. Everything was quite alarming enough without ghosts coming into it.

Bother Dad for taking this job, I thought. I could be in England, just coming home from school, hurling my bag across the floor to hit the radiator . . .

THE DARKSIDE GUIDE TO THE KINGDOM OF DOUME

BALDRIC THE ILL-OMENED

*Born in England sometime around 1130, Baldric acquired his name when his local church tower fell down the day he was knighted. He joined the other leading Knights of Doume (**Amalric the Aimless, Baldwin the Odd, Bohemond the Craven and William Le Thug**) to go on crusade out of boredom. The crusaders left England in good order, but lost their way once they got across the channel. The knights never reached their destination as Baldric met a gypsy while crossing the Carpathians who told him he would be doomed if he went to Jerusalem. Neither Bohemond nor Amalric objected when they stopped in Doume, although William Le Thug said it was rather too peaceful for his taste. Lacking anything better to do they overthrew the local rulers, the House of Ghoulburg, and built their own castles to oppress the peasants. Baldric died in 1210 when a volume of the **Prophecies of Ill Repute** fell on his head in the Black Library of Castle Scuttle. He was not mourned by the native Doumians.*

Twenty-Six

I WAS RIGHT TO BE WORRIED ABOUT WILF. WHAT neither Foujay nor I knew at the time was that while we were junketing across the Doumian landscape in trams and trains, Wilf and Hardhat had been taken prisoner.

They were, in fact, incarcerated within the grim black walls of Castle Scuttle.

Their first mistake on arriving at Scuttle had been to stop and ring us on the mobile while we were at the monastery. If they hadn't done that, they wouldn't have lost sight of Rudi D. And, more importantly, they wouldn't have lost sight of Mr Johnson.

By the time they'd crossed over on the footbridge to the Loop line and out of the station, the others had vanished.

'How?' said Wilf, looking around him in disbelief. He looked up and down the dusty track; as I said, you could see a long way in both directions. Empty. Not a soul in sight.

Then, a little further along the road, a dark shape emerged from the rough grass on the side and slithered across the road.

'One of the Scuttle snakes,' said Hardhat knowledge-ably. 'There are a lot of them about here. Black and purple markings. Some people keep them as pets, but I wouldn't. They're poisonous.'

Wilf didn't have a snake phobia, but he did feel that poisonous snakes didn't add much to the attractions of Scuttle. Then he pricked up his ears, and listened hard.

'They grow quite big,' went on Hardhat.

'Ssh,' said Wilf. 'I can hear a car. Very faint, and in the distance.'

'Car!' said Hardhat. 'That's why we can't see them.'

'Someone must have had a car waiting at the station. It makes sense, since I don't think there'll be many buses in this kind of place.'

'One a day in each direction,' said Hardhat helpfully.

Wilf was thinking hard. 'It would account for Rudi D., maybe, and Stuka's men might have gone with him, but where's Mr Johnson? Or, if it's Johnson's car, where are the others? It's unlikely that they've all gone off in the same car.'

Hardhat thought about that for a bit. He rubbed his nose with his forefinger, always a sign of concentration with Hardhat. 'Unless they've arrested Mr Johnson,' he said in a flash of inspiration. 'Then he'd be with them. Handcuffed, you see.'

'Ah,' said Wilf. 'That's probably what's happened. Thank goodness for that. We can't follow them if they're in a car, not out here.'

'Should have brought my blades,' said Hardhat.

'On this track?' said Wilf scornfully. 'When's the next train back?'

'Won't be for two hours,' said Hardhat. 'The train we got off goes to the border, hangs about a bit, and then comes back on the return journey. Single line, you see.'

'I'm not staying here in this dismal station for the next two hours,' said Wilf. 'Let's go that way, towards that gloomy old wreck of a castle, and see what we can find.'

'I'll report to Foujay,' said Hardhat.

If Hardhat had managed to get through, it could all have gone very differently. As it was, he must have rung just as the train was in a tunnel, because Foujay's phone didn't give a single beep.

They set off down the track towards the castle, feeling a sense of relief now that their tracking activities were over. They were careless, Wilf admitted afterwards, and they never saw Johnson slip out from behind the elder tree in front of the station and set off after them on stealthy feet.

Twenty-Seven

WILF TOLD ME THAT HE THOUGHT SCUTTLE WAS the most depressing place he'd seen in Doume. I pointed out that he hadn't seen much at all of Doume, but he said he'd been looking out of the train windows, and Scuttle definitely scored nil on any worth-a-detour chart.

I tended to agree with him, going by the little I saw of it. It wasn't exactly the village that was so awful; it was tiny, apart from anything else, with just a handful of houses and a shop on the corner of the crossroads in the centre of the village.

No, it was the brooding presence of the castle that cast a shadow over the whole place. And there was nobody about as Wilf and Hardhat reached the village. That was because it was a holiday, no doubt. All the inhabitants must have been indoors watching football in the dark or off cluttering up roads and trains on their way to see family and friends.

Wilf and Hardhat walked through the village and on up the track towards the towering castle entrance. Above the massive, fortified gateway was carved a huge bat, and looking up you could see the remains of a portcullis.

'I don't like this place,' said Hardhat as they walked on through the gateway. 'Fancy living here, ugh.'

Wilf was examining a faded list of names on a board by the arch which led into the central courtyard. 'Looks as though it's been used for workshops or businesses,' he said. 'It says Snood Sanitaryware, that's the firm that made all the things in our bathroom.'

'That's right,' said Hardhat. 'I remember coming here with my dad when I was small. He was collecting some items to smuggle across the border. They had a china company here, with kilns and everything. And there were some glass-makers as well.'

'Shall we go on?' asked Wilf, but Hardhat was already halfway across the courtyard. He was heading for a wide flight of steps towards another massive door, which stood half-open, creaking in an unnerving way.

The door led into a huge hall, full of shelves on which stood dusty boxes and the odd contorted glass jug or cracked bowl. Underfoot was a carpet of broken glass.

'There are glass-makers here, too,' said Hardhat, after some thought.

'Watch where you're walking,' Wilf said. 'You don't want spikes of glass in your trainers. It's all over the place.'

'I knew I should have brought my blades,' said Hardhat.

'Don't you ever have more than one thought in your head?' said Wilf, exasperated.

'It's easier that way,' said Hardhat. 'What a dump this is.'

For the second time that afternoon, Wilf stopped to listen. Hardhat stared at him. 'What now? Ghosties on the landing?'

'I can hear music,' said Wilf. 'I'm sure I can.'

'What kind of music?' said Hardhat.

'Old tunes. Drippy, soupy stuff. It's what Mrs Cavity listens to on the radio all day.'

If Wilf hadn't been listening so hard to the music, he would have heard the footsteps creeping up behind him.

As it was, he whirled round too late. Hardhat might have put up a fight, but he'd been expertly tripped up, and he was too busy trying to escape from the broken glass to be any use.

Handcuffed together, they were pushed out of the hall, across a wide passage, and thrust through an arched door.

It shut behind them with a loud bang, and they could hear bolts being drawn across on the other side.

'Oh, great,' said Wilf, who found himself being hauled by Hardhat over to the small patch of light which came through a narrow slit high up in the dark stone wall.

'Let's get these off,' said Hardhat, setting to work on the handcuffs.

'The point of handcuffs is that you can't get them off,' began Wilf.

Click.

'Well, you aren't supposed to be able to get them off.'

'The police ones usually come off if you know how,' said Hardhat. 'They buy rejects from Romania. None of them work properly. Sometimes, if you're unlucky, you get the ones that won't ever come off. Not with a key or anything. And it's difficult to cut through a handcuff.'

Wilf was thankful that they'd had the other sort.

Gradually their eyes got used to the dim light, and they began to take in their surroundings.

'Hardhat,' said Wilf, after a while. 'Um, what are all these?'

Hardhat pursed his lips and whistled tunelessly as his eyes flickered along the shelves.

'Hands,' he said at last. 'With a bit of arm attached.'

He reached up and plucked one down. 'They're made of clay. This must be a line from the pottery, perhaps this is a store. They make souvenirs.'

'Souvenirs? Who'd want a hand?'

'They painted them, bit of grey, bit of blood, some nasty fingernails stuck on and you'd leave it in a door or on a bookcase, something like that.'

'Why?'

'As a joke?' suggested Hardhat. 'Or to scare your friends, perhaps. I don't think they sold very well. That's why there are so many of them here.'

'How come you know all this?' asked Wilf, looking at Hardhat with new respect.

'My uncle deals in souvenirs. But he goes in for things that people want. Skulls are much more popular than hands.'

'That one up there looks different,' said Wilf, pointing.

Hardhat squinted up into the darkness and then hooked it down.

'Must have had a line in mummified hands,' he said. 'This isn't china. It must be plastic, or polystyrene.'

'It's very realistic,' said Wilf, handling it gingerly before putting it down on a nearby shelf. 'Finger-prints and everything. You'd almost say it was a real hand. Ugh. Whoever would buy a thing like that? It's disgusting.'

Twenty-Eight

B EEP.

'Good,' said Foujay, pulling out the mobile phone. 'Hardhat and Wilf back in contact. Wilf? Is that you? Where are you?'

Crackle, hiss, whine. That didn't sound very promising to me.

'Hardhat! Can you hear me?' Foujay gave the phone a sharp tap. 'Do you think the battery's running down?'

'It tells you if it is,' I said, taking it from him and having a look. 'No, the battery's fine. They must be somewhere where the signal's weak or cut out. On a train, maybe.'

'Hmm,' said Foujay. His eyes narrowed as he looked up at the grim castle which towered over the village. 'What about in there? Would a signal get through those walls?'

'I shouldn't think anything would get through those walls. But why should Wilf and Hardhat be in there?'

'They must be somewhere here,' said Foujay. 'They wouldn't catch a Loop train, because it wouldn't take them back to Valderk. They'd have to wait for the one they got off to come back on its return trip.'

'Why should they have come this way?'

'Wouldn't you?'

Foujay was right. I couldn't see Wilf taking to the hills for a country ramble. Wilf is not one of life's nature-walkers. Wilf likes civilization. Although, as we set off for the castle entrance, and I saw the stone walls looming darkly above our heads, I didn't reckon that Castle Scuttle and civilization had much to do with each other.

We had just gone through the first archway when we heard a car. Foujay stopped, and looked round. 'Into the shadows,' he said. 'Quick.'

We lurked as a police car, driven by Rudi D., shot past.

'Funny,' said Foujay, stepping out into the gateway. 'Stuka's men aren't in the car, nor Mr Johnson. I wonder what he's done with them.'

There was a squeal of brakes, and we jumped back as a much bigger and faster car hurtled up the slope and shot through the entrance.

'Wow,' said Foujay. 'Stuka. Let's see what's up.'

He set off at a run.

I followed, not caring at all about Rudi and Mr Johnson and Stuka and the Secret Police stooges. 'What about Wilf and Hardhat?'

'I expect they're hot on the trail.'

We whizzed round a corner and then did the flatten-and-lurk bit again as we saw Rudi D. just ahead of us, standing in front of a bolted door.

'Funny,' I whispered in Foujay's ear. 'I'm sure I can hear Wilf and Hardhat shouting from inside there.'

'Why doesn't he open the door and let them out?' said Foujay, darting forward as Rudi D. made off along the dark passage and disappeared up a flight of steps.

We listened at the door. It was very thick, and you couldn't hear anything clearly, but there was definitely someone in there. 'Could be the entrance to a dungeon,' said Foujay, hanging back. 'That could be ghostly cries from past inhabitants.'

'Oh, pooh,' I said, tugging at the bolts. 'Nothing

ghostly about that. I tell you, Wilf and Hardhat are locked in there.'

'Thank goodness for that,' said Wilf as the door finally opened and he and Hardhat tumbled out.

'Who locked you in there?'

'Mr Johnson,' said Wilf.

'Don't know why,' said Hardhat, swinging the extra hand he was holding.

'What a horrible thing,' I said with a shudder.

'Do you think so?' said Hardhat. 'I quite like it. I think it's meant to look historic. I'm going to hang it on my wall.'

Oh, well, we don't all have the same tastes, I suppose.

Foujay was already creeping up the stairs. We joined him at the corner of a long gloomy room with pillars holding up a distant roof. The entrance where we were standing was in one corner, and another flight of stairs led down into the room.

'Empty,' said Foujay. 'We'll try over there.'

'No,' said Wilf. 'I can hear that music again.'

Music? What was he on about? Still, Wilf has the sharpest ears out. If he said he could hear music, then he could.

'This is no time for music,' said Foujay severely.

'Where there's music, there'll be people,' said Wilf, setting off purposefully across the room.

Foujay shrugged. 'Okay,' he said. 'But I still think we'd do better to find Rudi D. He'll be right where the action is. Cornering Johnson at this very minute, I wouldn't be surprised.'

We'd reached what must have been the great hall of the castle, and a terrible place it was, too. Ancient suits of armour leant against the walls, looking as if they were about to get up and go. Faded banners flapped overhead. A big poster had been stuck up between two of the high narrow windows, and although it was tattered and torn, you could still read what it said.

'Forward, Workers of Doume.'

A gallery ran round the hall, just below the slitted windows.

'Look,' said Hardhat.

We looked.

'Mr Johnson,' said Foujay as a figure in a white mac ran along the gallery. 'I knew it.'

He was followed by a tall thin man in glasses. 'Rudi D.,' I said.

After him, getting up a good speed, came a burly type in shades. 'Stuka,' said Hardhat in tones of foreboding.

'After them,' said Foujay, heading for the great stone spiral staircase which twisted up from a turret in the corner of the hall.

As we ran along the gallery, we looked down to see the three of them running after each other across the hall below.

'Back down,' panted Foujay.

'I know where Johnson's going,' said Wilf. 'Follow me.'

Twenty-Nine

IF YOU COULD TAKE OUT A PATENT ON KEEN HEAR-
ing, Wilf would make a fortune.

He led us through Castle Scuttle like a ship following
radar signals. It wasn't long before we could all hear the
music, but it was Wilf who could tell exactly which
direction it was coming from, and which passage or
steps to take to keep us on a steady course towards the
source of the jazzy thumps.

As we bolted along, Foujay was muttering to himself.
Then, as we turned a particularly sharp corner, he
stopped, quite suddenly.

Hardhat and I cannoned into him, and Wilf turned
round to see what the noise was.

'Why did you do that?' I said.

'Hardhat, let me look at that hand.'

'Hand?'

'Not yours, the one you're carrying.'

'I'm keeping it.'

'I just want to look at it.'

We had stopped by one of the larger window slits, and
Foujay carried it over, setting it down on the wide
slanting ledge to get a closer look at it.

'We're wasting time,' said Wilf.

'No, we aren't,' said Foujay. 'Do you know what this
is?'

'A horrible model of an old hand,' I said.

'This,' said Foujay, with a dramatic flourish of the nasty limb, 'is none other than the Hand of the Knight of Doume.'

'The hand of Doume?' said Wilf.

'The one that was stolen from the cathedral?'

'The mummified one?'

'Yes,' said Foujay triumphantly. 'And look.' He held the hand and pressed its fingers down into the dust which was heaped up on the ledge.

We crowded round to look.

Unbelievable. There, in the dust, was a perfect set of fingerprints.

'What does it mean?' said Wilf.

'Think about it,' said Foujay. 'This case is littered with fingerprints.'

That was true enough. Fingerprints at the scene of the thefts, fingerprints at the monastery . . .

'All the same. And all made by this,' said Foujay. 'I bet you anything you like. It was to make sure the criminal could never be identified. And, I bet, to make the investigator look stupid.'

'So the fact that Johnson's fingerprints didn't match meant nothing.'

'Who else, apart from criminals and suspects, have their fingerprints on record?' asked Foujay. 'You two should know that. Your dad would.'

I had no idea, but Wilf's busy brain was whirring into action. 'Police officers,' he said. 'So that if they leave prints while they're investigating, those ones can be ignored.'

I was none the wiser. 'What does it matter? We know Johnson's the thief.'

Wilf pricked up his ears, but this was a sound we could all hear. Footsteps. Running footsteps, gaining on every step.

Foujay picked up the Hand of Doume and set off at a cracking pace. 'Don't get caught,' he shouted over his shoulder. 'Or we'll probably all be shut up in another storeroom.'

We were running towards the music, and the sounds of trumpet, clarinet, piano and bass were getting louder and louder. We were darting down passages and running through what must once have been bedrooms. We seemed to have lost our pursuer, as we could no longer hear footsteps at our back. Relieved, we slowed down.

'Some amplifier, that,' said Wilf breathlessly. 'And the echoes are tremendous in a castle.'

A few more rooms, a long passage, and we had reached the source of the noise. We all slid to a halt outside another heavily barred door.

'What?' said Foujay.

'That's odd,' said Hardhat.

'I wonder why?' said Wilf.

I just stood and stared. Above the door were bars running in both directions. Hanging on a hook by the bars and turned to blast through them was a loudspeaker. It was attached to a cassette player set on the floor.

The jazz was blasting our eardrums; it must have been mind-boggling to anyone inside the room.

'Turn it off,' I shouted, and Hardhat gave the cassette player a neat kick. It gave a gulp, and the din stopped.

What a relief.

A voice came from inside the room. 'Let me out, you villain. I will never do what you want, I will never reveal the secret of the formula.'

'Well I'm blowed,' said Foujay. 'It's Cousin Long-fang.'

'Hi, Coz,' he shouted through the door. 'It's Foujay here. Hold on, we're going to open this door.'

Thirty

HARDHAT'S HEFTINESS WAS COMING IN HANDY.
The iron bar across the door was very heavy, and then, after we'd shifted it, it took a lot of effort to draw back the heavy bolts on the top and bottom of the door.

I don't know how I'd pictured Longfang. Friar Tuck with gout, perhaps. I almost burst out laughing when I saw him as we fell into the room. There were several steps leading down from the door.

In fact, he was exactly like Foujay, only older. The same sharp but merry eyes, exactly the same colouring. And the only difference in their hair was that Longfang's was grey, and he had a monkish tonsure on the top of his head.

'Bah,' he said by way of greeting. 'Semolina! Have you got any chocolate?'

I wondered for a moment if he'd gone mad, imprisoned in ghastly Castle Scuttle, but then I realised my mistake. He was talking about the bowl of cold semolina pudding which sat, untouched, on the table, with an unused spoon beside it.

For those of you who have never seen or tried to eat semolina, I will describe it. It's a sloppy, slimy, grainy pudding made with milk. Some people like it; I don't. And it was clear that Longfang shared my dislike.

'Poor Longfang,' said Foujay, trying not to laugh. 'He's a famous gourmet, you know.'

'Torturing me,' said Longfang. 'Blasting that terrible music through the door, hour after hour. And offering me nothing to eat except that pudding. I'll sue, that's what I'll do once I'm out of here.'

Wilf had been digging about in his pockets. He had unearthed a few squares of chocolate, and giving them a quick wipe with the corner of his shirt, he handed them over to Longfang.

'Thank you,' he said, giving the chocolate a good sniff. 'Ah, at least seventy per cent cocoa solids. A chocolate-eater of discernment, I can tell.' And the chocolate was gone in a flash.

Hardhat nipped up the steps. 'Company on its way,' he shouted.

'Pass the iron bar in,' said Foujay. 'We may need to defend ourselves.'

I had spotted an ancient-looking piece of parchment on the table near the semolina. 'Hey,' I said. 'Is that the secret formula?'

'Yes,' said Foujay, scooping it up, and tucking it into his belt.

'The scoundrel who kidnapped me was trying to force me to translate it for him,' said Longfang indignantly. 'He's got all kinds of dictionaries and so on to help with the translation. Huh. They wouldn't be any use to him, the formula is far too specialised. And I wouldn't need them. I can read Doumian as easily as any of the other sixteen languages I know.'

'Johnson,' cried out Hardhat. 'Here comes Johnson.'

'The criminal,' I said.

'And Rudi D. coming into the last bend now,' sang Hardhat.

'Hot on the trail,' I said. Longfang would surely be

able to identify Johnson, and that would be the end of the case.

'I'm afraid I couldn't possibly identify the man who dragged me here,' said Cousin Longfang. 'He wore a hood over his head, and must have had a handkerchief in his mouth, for he mumbled terribly. I couldn't understand a word he said. Then he chloroformed me, and I woke up here, with him going on at me from the other side of the door. No, no, I can tell you nothing about him.'

'No need,' I said as Johnson came into the room. 'Where's Rudi Drinkwater?' he said, his eyes darting suspiciously round the room as though we'd hidden the detective under the table.

'Coming along behind to arrest you,' I burst out. 'We know what you've been up to. We know you stole the Hand of Doume, and used it to make all those fingerprints, and that means you're guilty of all the other thefts as well.'

'What? Me? I did nothing of the kind. The reason I want to get hold of Rudi Drinkwater is to ask him to get all these people off my back. I'm entirely innocent, and I can't do my work if I'm followed everywhere I go by Stuka's men.'

'What do you expect?' I said.

Mr Johnson paid no attention.

'And you've been following me as well,' he said, turning on Hardhat and Wilf. 'I locked you up, and I don't know how you got out. But just leave me alone, will you?'

Rudi D. stood at the entrance, one hand behind his back. He looked round the room, a faint smile at the corner of his thin lips. 'Well, well, well,' he said. 'What a surprise.'

Stuka came thundering up from behind him. Rudi D. stepped neatly to one side and Stuka hurtled down the steps.

I was watching Johnson, worrying that he might make a bolt for freedom.

'It isn't Johnson you've got to watch,' Foujay hissed into my ear.

'Why not?'

'He was out of the country when the Hand of Doume was stolen, I've only just remembered. He can't have taken it. He was in England for three months, and only came back when you did.'

'Then who . . .?'

At that moment, Rudi D. swung his hand out from behind his back.

We froze.

In his hand was the kind of thing you see in museums: a mace, black, evil and horribly spiked. He gave it an experimental swing or two, and we all backed away. Stuka, after a momentary bluster, tried to take cover behind Hardhat. What a coward.

'Don't you back away,' Rudi D. said to Longfang. 'You're coming with me. Once we're across the border, I'm sure I will be able to make you see sense.'

'You haven't got the formula,' said Hardhat. 'So it's no good taking him.'

Rudi D. sneered. 'Idiot,' he said. 'I have a copy, do you think I'm that stupid. Now,' he said to Longfang, 'either you come with me willingly, or I'll tread on your gouty toe.'

Longfang gave a cry of anguish and limped towards the steps. Rudi D. leant down to grab a handful of red habit. 'Off we go,' he said in a silky voice which sent shivers down my spine.

'You aren't going anywhere,' said a voice from outside, and Rudi D. toppled forwards, stunned by a blow from a handbag.

Lulu stood in the doorway. 'Stop cowering there,

Stuka. Your men are coming now, so they can arrest the right man for once.'

Mr Johnson had kicked the mace out of Rudi's reach and Hardhat was standing over him, the iron bar held threateningly in both hands.

Lulu tripped down the steps. 'So much for all that karate training your department is supposed to do,' she said to Stuka.

'Um,' said Stuka.

There was the sound of sturdy boots echoing through the castle. 'Stuka's people,' said Johnson. 'Stuka, what are you going to charge Rudi with?'

Rudi, who had come round, struggled to sit up, glowering all the while at Lulu.

'Um,' said Stuka again.

'I'll tell you,' went on Lulu. 'Mutilating and stealing an ancient monument. That's the Hand of Doume. Stealing the Zizzo formula and planning to take it out of the country. That's another ancient treasure, and it's economic terrorism as well. I'm not sure you can get him on all the other thefts, not unless you can trace the stolen goods back into his possession. A clever lawyer will be able to explain away the fingerprints.'

'Talking of lawyers,' said Rudi sulkily. 'I demand to see mine, and I'm not saying another word until I do.'

'Aren't you?' said Stuka menacingly. 'We'll see about that.'

'Now, Stuka,' said Lulu calmly. 'You aren't working for your old masters any more. Be very careful, or those reporters from *The Daily Doume* and *The Shout* will have your guts for garters.'

'Reporters,' said Stuka furiously. 'Throw them all in the dungeons, that's what I say.'

Thirty-One

WHILE ALL THIS WAS GOING ON, WILF AND FOUJAY had been whispering together. I was straining to listen to what they were saying, but couldn't hear it above the rest of the conversation, and the loud stampings from Stuka's men as they set to work with the handcuffs. At first, they only succeeded in handcuffing two of their own group together, but they finally managed to attach a pair to Rudi.

'He'll be out of those in a trice,' warned Hardhat. 'If I can get out of them, so can he.'

Rudi glared at Hardhat and after some hasty consultation one of the Secret Police produced a length of rope, and they bound Rudi's hands together rather tighter than he cared for.

'Not like that,' he snarled. 'What a bunch of incompetents your people are, Stuka. I wouldn't employ any of them even as cleaners on my side of the service.'

'You haven't got a service at all now,' said Lulu. 'So pipe down.'

He was led grumbling away, and the others made to follow. I noticed that Foujay and Wilf were hanging back and making signs to me and Hardhat to do the same.

'What's up?' I said.

'Wilf reckons there's a fair chance that Rudi's stashed the other things away here in Castle Scuttle. It's obviously where he kept the hand all along, nobody would notice it here. Let's go and see if we can find anything else.'

Foujay set off at a rapid pace in the opposite direction to the prisoner's party, and we soon found ourselves back in the Snood part of the castle. 'Right, fan out,' said Foujay in his bossy way. 'We're looking for a biggish painting, a gold cup decorated with various beasts, a heap of wooden carvings, and a stone split down the middle. Oh, yes, and some fusty old books.'

'Like this one?' asked Hardhat, who'd been rummaging around in a dark corner. He held up a large, leather-bound book. 'And there's this here, as well. I don't know what it is.'

'A rolled-up canvas,' said Wilf at once. 'Let's have a look.'

You never saw such a terrifying picture in all your life. I will not describe it in detail, because even in our modern and enlightened world, well used to scenes of violence, the Doumian end of St Vlad is too horrible to relate. 'Ugh,' I said. 'Do roll it up again, Wilf.'

Wilf was hunting further, and he unearthed a golden bowl, thick with typical Doumian figures wound round the stem and the handles: evilly grinning, nightmare beasts.

'Isn't it wonderful?' said Foujay. 'One of the great treasures of Doume. Is the Craque of Doume there, too?'

It was, although it didn't look anything to get excited about, just a smooth, bluish-coloured stone with a wide crack down it. 'Damaged,' I said.

'No, no,' said Hardhat. 'It's always been like that. I had to draw it when I was at junior school, from a photo.'

'That's why it's called the Craque,' said Foujay knowledgeably. 'From the French. It's very old, centuries and centuries. They say that if it ever splits completely in two, Doume will fall.'

Fall where? I wondered.

The carvings from the King's Palace were there as

well, big, heavy things, full of awkward, spiky bits. We gave those to Hardhat to carry, gathered up the rest of the goodies and headed for the castle entrance to show our treasures.

Stuka immediately took charge of them, and we could see who was going to get the credit for finding them.

'Well done,' said Mr Johnson loudly. 'I'll see that your part in their recovery is recognized.'

That earned him a nasty look from Stuka. I was beginning to suspect that Mr Johnson was more than just an employee of a confectionery firm. When I said this to Foujay later, he agreed, and we came to the conclusion that Mr Johnson had all along been working for the government. 'Or an insurance firm, more likely,' was what my father said. 'I believe that the monastery, which has a lot more business sense than the rest of them, had insured the Craque.'

Lulu had had enough of all this. 'Now come along, Stuka,' she said firmly. 'If you've got your car, we can be on our way. The Secret Police can take those objects back to Valderk, there are enough of them for the treasures to be safe. You can call off those roadblocks now, and when we get back from our weekend you can arrange about a reward for Foujay and the others. Without them, I dare say that Rudi and Longfang – and the formula – would be on their way to the border.'

'Quite right,' said Mr Johnson. 'I say, I'm sorry I locked you up. I didn't know whose side you were on.'

'A reward,' said Lulu. 'And the order of St Vlad, second class, at the very least.'

Stuka was getting back his cool. 'Third class,' he said. 'Now, down to the car. The press must be told that the case is solved, the Hand of Doume has been found, the criminal arrested and that, once again, SKULK has triumphed.'

What a nerve.

'Never mind,' said Mr Johnson. 'I'll buy you all a Zizzo when we get back to Valderk. Let's hurry, the train's due.'

We hurried, and just caught it. As it rattled along towards the centre, we discussed why Rudi had stolen the things he had. It seemed a strange collection, and why hadn't he spirited them out of the country and sold them, if it was money he was after?

'He took them to confuse the issue,' said Johnson. 'The one thing he really wanted was the formula. He could sell that easily enough, and then he'd have stacks of money and he'd get his own back on Doume.'

'But he's a Doumian,' I protested. 'Why would he want to ruin his own country?'

'Ah, because he considered it had never appreciated his genius, and he bitterly resented the way Stuka took control of all the investigations, and took all the credit for any successes. Professional jealousy, you could say.'

'Well, I'm glad he didn't get away with it. Doume needs its Zizzo,' Mind you, I did feel a little sorry for Rudi, and he had been very clever, using that hand to make all those misleading fingerprints. 'What will happen to him?'

'Oh, he'll be sentenced to about a hundred years in prison, and Stuka will demand that the old salt mines be opened up for him to serve his term there. He'll spend a year or two incarcerated in the Palace prison, I should think, and then they'll let him out.'

'What?'

'Oh, yes. It's very expensive to keep people in prison, you have to feed them and provide clothes and so on. In Doume, they're generally let out pretty quickly these days, unless they're dangerous.'

'Goodness, what will Rudi do when he comes out?'

'Set up as a security consultant, I shouldn't be

The Daily News, London

Zizzo zafe and zound

From our correspondent in Valderk, Doume

Relief is univesal in the tiny Kingdom of Doume today following the news that the secret formula for the world-famous soft drink, Zizzo, has been recovered. Chief of Police Stuka followed a complex trail of theft to uncover the criminal (who has not been named).

His men traced the thief to a remote castle not far from the capital, Valderk. They also found a missing monk, many vanished national treasures, and the Hand of Doume. This is being reattached to its knightly owner by a team of top surgeons from the Hospital of Vlad the Reckless.

The Doumian economy – a report from our financial experts, *Money section p.1*

Doume – an unusual place for a holiday, *Travel section p.8*

Valderk named as City of Culture, *Magazine, p.5*

Is Zizzo good for you? Our panel does a testing taste, *Weekend section p.2* surprised,' said Mr Johnson. 'He could team up with your father, and sell his services to Zizzo Inc. You wait, we haven't heard the last of Rudi Drinkwater; you can be sure of that.'

The Daily Doume

Rudi Drinkwater, pipped to the post in solving the crime of the century by Chief Stuka, is to retire, it was announced today. He has been awarded the cross of Bane the Unholy (2nd class).

The Shout of Doume

Stuka triumphs again. Summons to palace for knees-up with King.

Comrade Vlad praises Stuka for brilliant detective work 'in the best tradition of our country'

The Shout says, Good for you, Stukie-baby

Stuka is travelling to France later this week for a holiday together with his constant companion, the lovely Lulu. We reckon he deserves it!

You will also enjoy from Elizabeth Pewsey
THE TALKING HEAD Trilogy

The Talking Head

'I don't make a habit of carrying anybody's head around. It's uncivilised.'

But Gilly and Hal, who inadvertently step through an arch and into a land outside time and space have to do exactly that. The head has red curls, green eyes and a difficult personality, and is accompanied by a tiresome talking raven. To get back to their own world, and to stop the Vemorians invading Tuan, they have to bury the head in the appointed place before the next full moon – and the head is distinctly unhelpful.

'This story is told with . . . the wit of Pat O'Shea's *The Hounds of the Morrigan* and older juniors might well enjoy the strangeness of the eerie flight and pursuit. *School Librarian*

The Dewstone Quest

'It's not the sort of thing you learn at school, making dragons laugh.'

When Ben vanishes in the fog, he finds himself in the strange world his friends Hal and Gilly have visited once before, called to fulfil a prophecy and find the Dewstone. But a lot of unpleasant people want to use the stone for their own ends – including the malicious Numens and foul cousin Erica.

With the dubious help of a spy, a Dollop, a touchy

dragon and an arrogant Immortal, among others, Hal and Gilly race to find Ben before his enemies do. But even if they succeed, Ben still has to make the right decision . . .

The Walled City

'Happen to have seen any bones?'
'Bones? Whose bones?
'Mine.'

Looking for Ivar's bones is the first task demanded of Scarlet when, fleeing through an arched doorway, she finds herself in the Walled City of soothsayers, outside time and the world she knows. Not until the end of a nightmare journey does she understand why she alone – a redhead like Ben who found the Dewstone – can release the myterious prisoner from Uthar's power and save the countries of Tuan and Vemoria from chaos and final destruction.